Deal. Bargain. Contract.

You are cordially invited
to the mutually beneficial wedding
of convenience between

Miss Rachel Hadley
and
Mr. Logan James

tomorrow at noon
in the courthouse
Billings, Montana

Please address questions and book requests to: Silhouette Reader Service
U.S.: 3010 Walden Ave., P.O. Box 1325, Buffalo, NY 14269
Canadian: P.O. Box 609, Fort Erie, Ont. L2A 5X3

Western Weddings

ELIZABETH AUGUST

THE COWBOY AND THE CHAUFFEUR

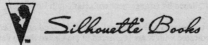

Published by Silhouette Books
America's Publisher of Contemporary Romance

SILHOUETTE BOOKS
300 East 42nd St.,
New York, N.Y. 10017

ISBN 0-373-30110-3

THE COWBOY AND THE CHAUFFEUR

Copyright © 1991 by Elizabeth August

Celebrity Wedding Certificates published by permission of Donald Ray Pounders from *Celebrity Wedding Ceremonies*.

A Letter from the Author

Dear Reader,

I'm so pleased to be a part of the Western Weddings series. For an author, when one of their books is out of print, it is as if a part of them is missing. I hope those of you who are reading *The Cowboy and the Chauffeur* for the first time will enjoy it as much as I enjoyed writing it. For those of you who read it several years ago, I hope you derive even more pleasure from it now than you did then. If this book brings a smile to your face or joy to your heart, then I have accomplished my goal.

Have a wonderful life and many, many happy endings of your own.

Best wishes,

Elizabeth August

To Marcia,
Thanks for the information about horses.
May you always remain firmly seated
in the saddle.

Chapter One

Rachel Hadley stood at attention beside the passenger door of the white Rolls-Royce. Stoically she ignored the passing glances of people going in and out of the busy airline terminal at Kennedy Airport. The fitted jacket and short straight skirt of her tailored gray uniform emphasized her full bust, femininely rounded hips and well-shaped legs. The matching gray high-heeled shoes added three inches to her five-foot-eight height, and her long, thick black hair hung in loose waves over her shoulders and down her back.

In contrast to the flagrantly sexy uniform and hairstyle, her makeup was demure. She wore pale pastel colors that blended with her ivory complexion. Then there was the way she wore her hat in a strictly businesslike manner. The steel-rimmed dark sunglasses that masked her green eyes also added a coolness to her appearance, and the firm set of her jaw warned, "Look but don't touch."

After working for Justin Parry for nearly five years, Rachel was certain that it was her cool but sexy appearance rather than her driving skill that had gotten her this job. Not that she wasn't an excellent driver; she was. But right from the beginning, she'd noticed the sparkle of amusement in Justin's eyes whenever he led a new acquaintance toward his car. And today was no exception. But it wasn't Justin she found her attention drawn to.

From behind the dark lenses of her sunglasses, she covertly studied the tall, muscular cowboy walking beside her employer. His name, Justin had informed her during the drive this morning, was Logan James.

Her employer was in the habit of leaving open the privacy window separating the passenger section of the car from the driver. He complained that at home, between his wife, daughter and granddaughter, he could never get a word in edgewise. So he talked to Rachel during their long drives between his estate on Long Island and his offices in Manhattan. Mostly he spoke about politics or some current news item that bothered him. Early on, Rachel had learned that he required no response from her, which was just as well, because she could only give him a fraction of her attention, anyway.

Most of her concentration had to remain on the
traffic through which he expected her to negotiate
without incident. They both knew she wasn't giving him her full attention, but that didn't trouble
him. On numerous occasions he'd praised her in a
good-humored, jesting manner of being such an
excellent listener. But this morning when he talked
about Logan James there had been an odd tone in
his voice that had caused her to give him more attention than usual.

As she listened to him, she'd wondered if he was
in awe of this cowboy or merely confused by Mr.
James's choice of life-style. "He owns a ranch in
Montana," Justin had told her. "Big place. Most
of it he leaves wild. He farms just enough of it to
keep his horses in feed. It's those horses that are his
real love. He breeds them, trains them and then
sells them. Makes a good living at it, too. But his
real money comes from gold. His grandfather
struck a rich vein, mined it and invested the money
wisely. Logan doesn't have to work a lick if he
doesn't want to. But the man sequesters himself up
there in the wilds and works his place himself."

Watching the rancher approaching the car,
Rachel's gaze traveled appraisingly over him. His
suit, a blue pin-striped single-breasted cut, was one
of the more expensive off-the-rack variety. His
western boots were finely tooled leather. They
added two inches to his height, she decided, guessing him to be around six foot three in his bare feet.

The Stetson he wore looked new. It was a blue that came close to matching the color of his suit. And, she noted with a twinge of surprise, he wore a normal tie with a blue-and-gray stripe instead of the string tie she'd expected. His shirt was white broadcloth.

His hair was thick and brown and a little on the shaggy side, but the style seemed to suit him. As for his face, he had a square jaw and a straight, medium-size nose. His mouth, which at the moment was formed into a polite smile, was nicely shaped for a man. The lips were not too thick, but not too thin, either. Actually, he had a very sensual mouth, she admitted. A long scar about the width of pencil lead trailed across his left cheek. It added a final touch of ruggedness to his features and produced the sort of face that fitted her image of what a cowboy should look like. All in all, he had an interesting face—not exactly handsome but intriguing enough to garner second glances from several of the passing females.

To her surprise, Rachel felt her blood flowing a little faster as the men came closer. Well, the cowboy *did* have a very masculine presence, she reasoned. Then he looked up and saw her, and his eyes narrowed. They were brown eyes, almost dark enough to be mahogany. And he was regarding her with a dubious look.

Apparently Mr. James was a chauvinist who didn't like the idea of being driven by a woman, she thought with amusement. But amusement was not the only thing she felt. Her blood seemed to flow faster still. Shaken by the reaction she was experiencing toward the cowboy, her back straightened even more.

Justin cast a bright smile in Rachel's direction. "Climb in," he encouraged his guest. "Rae's as good a driver as you'll find in New York or anywhere else on the East Coast for that matter."

"I'm sure she is," Logan replied in a slow drawl. Still, he hesitated a moment longer as his gaze flickered over her. "I'm just not used to having women hold doors open for me." Then with a polite smile that did not reach his dark eyes, he tipped his hat toward her and climbed into the Rolls.

Rachel had undergone numerous male scrutinies, usually of a much longer duration. But in that one quick glimpse she felt as if this Logan James had seen every inch of her. And was unimpressed, she concluded from the coolness in his manner.

Whether she impressed or did not impress one of Justin Parry's acquaintances had never concerned her before. She had a hard-and-fast rule about not socializing with her passengers. Although Justin had never said so, she knew he would not approve and her job would be in jeopardy. But in this instance, Rachel could not help feeling piqued. *It was the way he dismissed my presence as if I was some kind of barely noticeable insect,* she told herself as she waited until Justin was seated and then closed the door. Who did this Logan James think he was, anyway? *Someone who had come to cut a half-million-dollar deal with my boss,* came the answer, and mentally she laughed at herself. A man with that kind of money would naturally find a female chauffeur uninteresting. After all, to him she was merely a servant.

Climbing in behind the wheel of the Rolls, she felt a prickling sensation at the back of her neck. Glancing in the rearview mirror, she saw Logan James watching her, a coldly calculating expression on his face. She'd trained herself never to react to looks or inspections by her passengers, but the cowboy's gaze felt so close to a physical touch it was unnerving. *He's probably worried I'll get us into an accident,* she judged dryly, trying to ignore the unexpectedly strong feelings she was having toward this man. But they were not easy to ignore. She shrugged as if trying to brush off his gaze. Almost immediately the prickling sensation disappeared. Glancing again into the rearview mirror, she noticed that his attention had returned to Justin.

The privacy window separating the front seat from the passenger section was still open and she heard Justin say with an edge of fatherly reprimand, "So you still haven't found yourself a wife?"

That doesn't surprise me, Rachel thought as she again glanced at her passengers in the mirror. Logan James's jaw had hardened into a grim line. What woman would want to live with a chauvinist like him?

Authority entered Justin's voice. "A man needs heirs."

A fresh rush of heat spread through Rachel, followed by a curious curling sensation in her abdomen. Shocked by her body's reaction, she narrowly missed hitting a taxi that had abruptly pulled out in front of her. Glancing again in the rearview mirror, she saw Logan turn and frown at the back of her head with an "I must have been nuts to get into a car with a woman driver" expression on his face before his attention returned to Justin. I couldn't possibly have the slightest desire to bear his children, she chided herself. Not only had she seen him for the first time just a few minutes ago, he most definitely wasn't making a favorable impression on her. Besides, she liked her life as it was now. Granted it got a little lonely once in a while, but she was comfortable and safe. Those were two qualities that had evaded her during her youth.

"It's hard to find a woman who's willing to put up with the isolation," Logan was saying, his tone as grim as the expression on his face.

"I suppose," Justin conceded, then added with a mild hint of irritation, "What you need is a woman who doesn't consider shopping her vocation and throwing parties her avocation."

A gleam of amusement suddenly shone in the cowboy's eyes and his face relaxed into a smile. "How are your wife and daughter?"

Rachel's heart gave an unexpected lurch. When he smiled a genuine smile, he actually looked handsome. *Concentrate on the traffic,* she ordered herself, returning her full attention to the road.

"And granddaughter," Justin amended with an exaggerated sigh, which the obvious pride on his face immediately negated. "All are as beautiful as ever and as quick to want to entertain. When they heard you were coming, they immediately planned a dinner party for tonight in your honor. I hope you don't mind."

"I'm always happy to please the ladies," Logan replied in an easy drawl.

The thought of his "pleasing the ladies" caused an unpleasant nudge in the pit of Rachel's stomach. Her hormones must be definitely out of whack today, she decided, unable to find any other reason for these continued disquieting reactions to the cowboy.

"Now, tell me about this business deal you think would interest me," Logan requested, turning the conversation toward the purpose for his visit.

Justin pressed a button causing the privacy window to close. Rachel didn't feel shut out. His business was not her business. She tried to focus her attention totally on the traffic, but the mention of the dinner party had struck a particularly unpleasant chord in her. Disgruntledly, she breathed a heavy sigh. Justin's wife, Harriet, was a charming woman. And Justin had been honest in describing her and their offspring as beautiful. Harriet Parry had been a natural blond. Her hair was now white but her blue eyes were as sparkling as ever and her classic features showed only a modicum of aging, thanks to a bit of plastic surgery. Her daughter and granddaughter had inherited her blond good looks, but not her pleasant personality. Deloras, the daughter, was somewhat spoiled and since her third divorce had become difficult and demanding toward the servants. The granddaughter, Marylin, was thoroughly spoiled. At twenty-two she still threw tantrums when things didn't go her way. Their behavior had made servants hard to keep. Because of this, Harriet had coerced Rachel into acting as one of the maids at the dinner party this evening. Just the thought made Rachel's feet hurt.

Again she glanced in the rearview mirror. It would be interesting to see how the cowboy behaved toward the socially prominent women who would be there. *He'll probably ooze with charm,* she speculated cynically.

Her speculation was incorrect, Rachel was forced to admit later that evening. Logan James was polite but reserved toward all the guests. He smiled a great deal but the smile rarely reached his eyes. It was as if he was studying those present from behind an invisible barrier he kept between them and him.

He'd recognized Rachel. She'd caught the momentary look of confusion in his eyes when he first noticed her. She was wearing a high-necked black dress, one size too large, gathered at the waist by the ties of a white, lace-edged apron. Her hair was pulled back into a severe, matronly style and her dark glasses were gone. It was obvious he knew he'd seen her before, but just couldn't remember where. In the next instant there had been a glimmer of surprise, then his expression had once again become shuttered and he'd returned his attention to the redhead who was talking to him.

That was twice now he'd acted as if she was less interesting than an insect. Her chin tilted up and her shoulders straightened. What he thought of her was totally unimportant, she assured herself. And he was definitely of no interest to her.

She noted, however, that the two women seated on either side of him clearly felt otherwise. Both, she knew, were single at the moment and both showed a marked interest in the cowboy. Again Rachel experienced a twinge of agitation as they flirted with him. She told herself this was only because she hated seeing women throw themselves at a man. Logan James, for his part, remained polite but indifferent. His manner seemed to encourage the women and they flirted even more zealously.

Angry with herself for allowing him to occupy so much of her thoughts, she ordered herself to ignore him. But again she found that was easier said than done. Periodically she felt a prickling on her neck similar to the one she had experienced in the car. However, when she glanced in his direction, his attention was always elsewhere. *I need a vacation,* she decided. Her nerves were so tense that she was imagining him watching her.

Finally the party moved from the dining room to the ballroom. A band had been hired to provide music for those who wanted to dance. Although Logan showed no inclination toward that activity, she noticed that, in addition to his two dinner partners, several of the other single women began to seek out his company. The silent, stoic type is always a challenge to some females, she knew, telling herself that she found this amusing. But she didn't feel amused. She felt irritated. *I'm just tired. It's been a long day, and my feet hurt.* She determined to keep her attention on her job and off the cowboy.

During dinner, she'd waited on the table, always standing at attention ready to aid in the service. And for the past hour, she'd been tending bar in the far corner of the ballroom. Her shoes were beginning to feel about four sizes too small. She was just about to slip them off and work barefoot when a male voice came from her right.

"Your turn for a break," Thomas Clancy, the Parrys' butler, said in his usual staid manner. "I'll take over the bar."

Rachel knew Clancy didn't trust or like her, and his judgmental attitude irked her. Admittedly her past wasn't perfect, but if Justin was willing to give her a chance to prove herself, that should have been good enough for the butler. And hadn't she proven herself to be a loyal and honest employee these past five years? She forced a smile. "It's all yours."

With her head held high, she strode out onto the back patio. It was early March. The weather this time of year could be either springlike or winter cold. It changed almost from hour to hour. This afternoon had been warm, but tonight was chilly. She shivered as she breathed in the fresh Long Island air. It was pleasant here on the spacious Parry estate, a big change from the New York City tenements where she'd grown up.

"A little nippy out here, isn't it?" Lyle Martin interrupted her thoughts.

Rachel turned to see the tall, handsome blond man approaching. He was her age, twenty-seven, but that was the only thing they had in common. He was a member of one of the socially prominent families here on Long Island. He'd attended Harvard and after graduating joined his father in their thriving investment business. At the moment he was dating Justin's granddaughter. "I needed a little fresh air," she replied.

He came up beside her and lifted his hand to trace the line of her jaw with the tip of his finger. "I think I like you better in your chauffeur's uniform." A gleam of mischief sparkled in his blue eyes. "Or maybe I'd like you even better in nothing at all."

Rachel's guard came up. She'd heard rumors about Lyle's womanizing. She'd also heard that he had a penchant for servants. But she wasn't interested in a one-night stand or risking her job for this blond Casanova. "I think you should be getting back inside before Marylin misses you," she suggested pointedly.

Ignoring the dismissal in her voice, he traced the line of her jaw once again. "Marylin is a child. You on the other hand are a woman—one with obvious experience. I like that."

Rachel took a step back out of his reach. "I resent your assumptions, and if you touch me again, you'll regret it," she warned frostily.

He grinned with boyish charm. "So you like to play hard to get. I've always enjoyed a challenge." Bridging the distance between them, his hands closed around her upper arms.

Well, she had warned him. Remembering what she had learned in her self-defense class, Rachel braced herself for the maneuver that would free her. But before she could act, out of the corner of her eye she caught a movement in the shadows to her right.

"I believe the lady asked to be left alone," a male voice drawled.

Lyle's hold on Rachel tightened painfully as he glared at the intruder. "It's impolite to eavesdrop."

"Where I come from, it's also impolite to force your attentions on a lady when she doesn't want them." Logan had approached them and his gaze flickered from Lyle's face to his hands on Rachel's arms, then back to his face. There was a warning in Logan's eyes.

"Lyle, I've been looking all over for you," a young woman's voice sang out cheerfully, followed by the sound of high-heeled shoes clicking against the flagstones.

As if he was touching something that had suddenly become scalding hot, Lyle released Rachel abruptly. But not abruptly enough, Rachel realized, and mentally groaned. Marylin had managed to get beyond the point where Logan's body shielded her view just in time to realize that Lyle had been holding on to Rachel. The jealous hatred in the girl's blue eyes warned Rachel that there was going to be trouble.

"I came out here for some fresh air and found Rachel and Logan talking," Lyle said quickly. "He was asking her about how she liked driving in the traffic on Manhattan when she suddenly said she felt faint. I grabbed her, hoping to keep her from falling."

"And how do you feel now?" Marylin asked icily, her gaze resting threateningly on Rachel.

"Still a little light-headed," Rachel replied. She didn't like validating Lyle's lie, but in this instance she decided it would be prudent.

"Then you had better retire to your room for the evening," Marylin ordered haughtily. "I'll tell Thomas you aren't feeling well."

Beneath her facade of composure Rachel seethed. Under normal conditions it irked her to be spoken to that way. With Logan James present, she found it humiliating. Well, she *was* a servant, she reminded herself. Besides, her feet did hurt and she wanted Marylin to buy Lyle's tale. Beating a retreat would make life a lot easier. "Yes, ma'am," she replied stiffly and turned to leave.

As she walked away, she heard Marylin saying pointedly, "Come along, Lyle."

"You know I'd follow you anywhere," he replied with the ardor of a committed suitor.

Now there was a man who could ooze charm, Rachel mused. Then she heard Marylin asking, "Are you coming, Logan?" An edge of impatience in the blonde's voice suggested she hadn't entirely believed Lyle's story. "Several of the women guests have been asking where you disappeared to."

"I just need a bit more fresh air," the cowboy replied. "I'm not used to crowds. I'll come back inside in a moment or two."

"I'm sure Logan can take care of himself," Lyle interjected, obviously determined to hold all of Marylin's attention. "The band is playing a waltz and you know how much I love to waltz with you," he finished, a seductive quality lacing his words.

"Just remember that it's *me* you like to waltz with," Marylin returned tartly, her words accompanied by the clicking of her heels as she moved across the patio toward the French doors that opened into the ballroom.

"Only you," Lyle assured her in his best soothing tone.

A prickling at the nape of Rachel's neck caused her to glance over her shoulder. Logan James was watching her, and her back straightened even more. She'd noticed the barely discernible raising of his eyebrow when she'd backed up Lyle's lie. Well, Mr. James's job hadn't been on the line.

She hated having to endure Marylin's little snits and putdowns, but Justin was a good boss. He paid her a decent salary, and the job included her meals and a furnished private apartment above the garage. Thus she had very few living expenses and she'd been able to save a large percentage of her pay. She'd been a fool to allow something as insignificant as a pass by Lyle Martin to get her fired.

A smile suddenly came to her face as she rounded the side of the house and was finally out of Logan's sight. In this instance, Marylin's little snit had a silver lining. It had gotten her away from the party. Now she could go to her room and get out of these shoes.

But a few minutes later as she kicked off the black pumps, a wave of apprehension washed over her. Frowning at herself, she shrugged it off. Even if Marylin didn't entirely buy Lyle's lie, all Justin's granddaughter could do was make Rachel's life a bit miserable for a couple of days. "And I've lived through worse than she can dish out," Rachel muttered, beginning to shed her clothes in preparation for a soothing hot shower.

Chapter Two

Idiot! Rachel mentally screamed at herself. She'd been a fool to underestimate Marylin. It was eight o'clock the next morning, and during the past hour Rachel's life had come crumbling down around her. She had been eating breakfast with the rest of the servants when Justin had strode into the kitchen with Marylin close behind. Coming to a halt at the table, he announced grimly, "My safe has been broken into and my wife's, my daughter's and my granddaughter's jewelry has been stolen."

Looks of shock showed on the faces of those present.

"I haven't called the police yet. Recovering the jewelry is more important to me than catching the criminal. There were several family heirlooms taken." Justin's gaze focused on Rachel. "I know everything was in the safe after our guests left, because I personally returned the jewels my wife, Deloras and Marylin had worn to the party." Accusation entered his voice as he continued to stare at Rachel. "Marylin has told me that she came down to the kitchen in the early-morning hours for a glass of milk and on her way back to her room, she thought she saw you leaving by the rear door. At the time, she didn't think anything of it. She just assumed you had left something in the main house and had come back to get it."

Clancy was looking at Rachel with an "I knew you couldn't be trusted" expression on his face.

Ignoring him, Rachel looked at Justin levelly. "I never came back to the main house last night."

"Then you won't object if I have Clancy search your room," he said, his voice carrying a challenge.

His distrust hurt. She'd thought she'd proven her loyalty during the past five years. Her back stiffened with pride. "I would prefer if you searched my room yourself," she said. "I've got nothing to hide."

The accusation in Justin's voice grew stronger. "I hope not. I gave you this job because I thought you deserved a chance. I had begun to believe I could trust you." He paused. "I'll accompany Clancy."

Rachel's stomach knotted. He'd already decided she was guilty. As she rose from the table she could feel the other servants watching her. Glancing at them, she realized that not one of them would come to her aid. Even those she had begun to think of as friends had a question in their eyes. *You should know better than to count on anyone to be on your side,* she chided herself curtly. Head held high, she led the way out of the kitchen and toward her apartment. Justin, Marylin and Clancy followed.

Reaching her rooms, she unlocked the door and stepped aside to allow the others to enter.

Justin gave Clancy a nod and the butler began his search.

Rachel's stomach knotted tighter. She knew Clancy wouldn't find anything, but even so that wouldn't prove her innocence. There were too many places on the estate where the jewels could be hidden.

The sound of footsteps on the stairs behind her caused her to glance over her shoulder. It was Logan James. Mentally she groaned. This was humiliating enough without having the cowboy as a witness.

Reaching the doorway, he stood beside her and surveyed the scene inside. It was a one-room apartment without any cooking facilities. The couch pulled out into a bed. Rachel kept her living quarters neat. When she left this morning, her bed had been turned back into the couch, the drawers of her bureau closed and the items in her closet carefully arranged. Now, with Clancy's search, the pillows from the couch lay scattered on the floor, the bed had been pulled out and the mattress was askew. The drawers in her bureau were open and the contents mussed. "Heard there was a lynch party going on up here," Logan drawled, his gaze coming to rest on Justin.

Rachel stared at him in disbelief. There had been disapproval in his voice as if he felt that what they were doing to her was wrong.

"It's perfectly reasonable for us to suspect Rachel," Marylin said quickly, her voice sticky sweet. "She has, after all, spent time in prison for robbery." She glanced petulantly at Justin. "My grandfather has a big heart. He was willing to give her a chance."

Logan's gaze swung to Rachel and she saw the sudden doubt in his eyes. Her back stiffened defensively. "I didn't take their jewels."

"We aren't here simply because of Rachel's past," Justin said. He glowered accusingly at her. "Marylin told me what happened last night on the patio."

His voice had an ominous quality. Rachel frowned anxiously. "What did she say happened?"

Justin's expression became grimmer. "She told me about finding you flirting with Lyle. It was obvious he was annoyed by your attention. She warned you that your job was in jeopardy if you behaved like that again, and you told her that you were getting bored here, anyway. You went even further and said that you were only waiting for the right moment to leave. At the time she didn't know what you meant. It's obvious now that you were only biding your time until you could take a few valuables with you."

"That's not what happened!" Rachel blurted out.

"Lying will do you no good," Justin admonished. "Remember, Lyle was a witness."

A feeling of helplessness washed over Rachel. Lyle was the kind of heel who would swear to anything Marylin said.

"That's not the way I remember it," Logan said, his gaze narrowing on Marylin. "As I recall, it was Lyle who made a pass at Rachel, and I don't recall Rachel saying anything about being bored with her job here and wanting to leave."

Rachel stared at the cowboy. He was actually willing to risk his friendship with Justin by coming to her defense. No one had ever jeopardized themselves for her before.

Marylin smiled catlike at Logan. "Of course you would say that. I suspected that after Lyle and I went back inside, she seduced you. After all, you never came back into the party." Her mouth formed a reprimanding pout. "I know you live like a hermit out there on your ranch, and the chance to share a bed with a woman must have been irresistible. But my grandfather is your host and an old friend. I can't believe you would lie to him like that."

Logan's jaw had hardened into an angry line. "I've got my faults, but lying isn't one of them."

Justin's gaze traveled from Logan to Marylin, who stood her ground, looking like an innocent who had been struck an unfriendly blow. Scowling, he turned back to Logan. "She's right. You never did come back into the party."

"I'd had a long day," Logan replied in something close to a growl. The fury in his eyes was evidence that he didn't like his word being questioned. "I took a short walk and then went to my room by the back stairs."

Clancy suddenly cleared his throat loudly as if preparing to make a profound announcement. Rachel turned toward him. The triumphant expression on his face caused a cold chill of apprehension to race down her spine. The butler had taken a shoe box out of the closet. A silence fell over the room as he reached into it and lifted out a handful of the stolen jewelry.

Rachel balled her hands into fists to keep herself from shaking outwardly. Pride wouldn't allow her to let the others see how frightened she was. Her gaze swung on Marylin, and she saw the sly smile that flashed across the woman's face. In that instant she knew the truth. It would have been easy for Marylin to get the spare key to this apartment, then use it and return it. "You planted those here,"

Rachel accused. "You're nothing but a spoiled brat. This is your way of getting even because your boyfriend made a pass at me."

Justin glared at Rachel. "I would suggest that you say nothing until you get a lawyer," he advised. "I'm going to call the police now. You will remain here in your room with Clancy guarding the door until they arrive."

Logan hadn't shown any reaction when the jewels had been found. Rachel glanced toward him expecting to see accusation in his eyes, but instead, his attention was on Marylin. "And what if I'm willing to swear," he said to Justin, "that not only did your granddaughter lie about the confrontation last night but that I saw her entering and leaving this room early this morning?"

Marylin paled. "You're nothing more than a boorish cowboy. Who would believe you? My grandfather has an impeccable reputation."

"And I'd hate to see that reputation smudged by a spoiled, vengeful female," Logan countered warningly.

Justin was looking at Marylin now. "I want the truth," he said curtly.

The wheedling, helpless-little-girl expression she used when she wanted to get her grandfather on her side spread over Marylin's face. "You know I would never lie to you, but I don't want a scandal. And this cowboy—" she tossed Logan a distasteful glance "—is obviously so smitten with Rachel he'll say anything to help her. Since we have recovered the jewels, I suggest we don't call the police. Just fire her and see that she never works in this city again."

The glimmer of anger in Justin's eyes revealed that he knew his granddaughter had lied. But when he turned toward Rachel, there was no apology on his face. "I think it would be best if you sought employment elsewhere, preferably in another city. I'll write you a letter of recommendation. For that, I expect this matter never to be discussed again," he said coldly. Then, motioning for Clancy and Marylin to precede him, he left the room.

"So much for justice," Rachel muttered as the three reached the bottom of the stairs. She had been standing on the small landing outside her room. Now she entered it, and her gaze traveled over the mess Clancy had left behind.

"What will you do now?"

Rachel glanced over her shoulder. Logan was leaning against the doorjamb watching her. She'd expected him to follow the others, maybe try to mend his bridges with Justin. "Leave town," she replied. She didn't like the idea of being run out by someone like Marylin Jennings, but Rachel was a practical woman. Marylin would make her life miserable if she stayed. Tears of hurt and disillusionment suddenly burned at the back of her eyes. "I thought I'd found a place for myself here. I thought Mr. Parry liked me and that he'd learned he could trust me." Realizing she had spoken in front of an audience, she stiffened with pride. A long time ago she'd begun hiding her true feelings from the world. It was much safer that way. Coolly, as if Justin's turning against her was of no deep or lasting concern, she added, "Of course no one should expect a job to last forever." Forcing the pain to the back of her mind, she remembered that she owed Logan her freedom. "I want to thank you. It was lucky for me that you saw Marylin this morning."

He shrugged. "Truth is I didn't see her."

Rachel studied him narrowly. "I thought you said you never lied." What really surprised her was that she'd believed him when he'd claimed to be a totally honest man. *I've watched one too many John Wayne movies,* she decided dryly.

He met her gaze levelly. "I didn't lie. I merely said, 'What *if* I was willing to swear...' I knew Marylin had lied about last night, so I figured you might be right about her planting the jewels here."

Technically, she conceded, he hadn't lied. Still, she continued to regard him skeptically. She found it hard to believe that this cowboy had come to her rescue. "Why would you risk your relationship with Justin for me?" she asked bluntly.

Contempt etched itself into his features. "I don't take well to being called a liar. As for Justin, any man who would let himself be manipulated by a woman is a fool. If he doesn't want to do business with me because I wouldn't let his granddaughter railroad an innocent person into jail, then that's fine with me."

There was strong disdain in his voice when he spoke of being manipulated by a woman. *Mr. James is clearly a man who lives his life on his terms and no one else's,* Rachel judged. That would explain why he didn't have a wife. She recalled that he'd given Justin some excuse about his ranch being too isolated for a female. More likely, it was his immovable attitude that kept him a bachelor.

"Speaking of jail," he said in a slow drawl, "did you really spend time in one?"

Rachel fought back a rush of embarrassment as she faced him squarely. Her past was her past. It couldn't be undone. "It was a home for delinquent girls. I took some money my mother and stepfather had stashed in the house. I figured at least part of it was mine. They didn't see it that way."

He raised a reproving eyebrow. "You stole money from your own family?"

He made it sound as if she was a callous ingrate. She told herself it shouldn't matter what he thought of her, yet it did. "My stepfather used to beat me," she heard herself saying in her defense. "He treated my mother like a queen and would make up stories about my behaving badly to justify his beatings. My mother took his side. I'm not sure she believed him, but she liked her life and I'd always been a nuisance to her." A bitter smile played at the corners of Rachel's mouth. "She wasn't exactly the nurturing type." Shrugging off the hurtful memories of her mother's rejection, she continued coolly, "One day when I was fifteen, I'd had all I could take. He started to hit me and I fought back. He fell and was knocked unconscious. I thought I'd killed him. I was scared. I took the money he and my mother kept stashed under their mattress and ran. A part of that money was what they'd made me give them from my baby-sitting earnings, so I figured at least some of it was mine, but they didn't see it that way. They called the police and had me picked up. I guess my stepfather had decided I'd gotten too big to knock around safely, so he had me prosecuted. He told the court I was incorrigible and dangerous and he had a black eye and broken arm to prove it. My mother agreed with him and the judge ruled against me."

Rachel had told her story before, but the telling had never felt so humiliating as it did at this moment. "I know taking the money wasn't right, but I learned my lesson." Unable to face Logan any longer, she let her gaze again travel around the room. The thought of how close she had come to going back to jail shook her, and the panic she had hidden so well earlier surfaced. "Thanks again for your help. I don't think I could have stood being confined again." Hearing herself make this admission aloud, she cringed inwardly. She didn't like allowing anyone to see her weaknesses. Her shoulders straightened and her voice became cool with command. "Now, if you'll excuse me, I've got some packing to do."

Ignoring the dismissal in her tone, he remained where he was. For a moment longer he regarded her in silence, then asked, "Can you cook?"

Surprised by this unexpected change in subject, she frowned at him. "Enough so that I won't starve."

His manner became businesslike. "I need a housekeeper. The woman who has been cooking and cleaning for me is pregnant. It's getting too difficult for her to take care of my house, as well as her own. If you want the job, it's yours. I'll match whatever Justin is paying you and you'll get room and board."

Rachel was dumbfounded. He'd offered her a job!

"You're only asking for trouble if you hire her." It was Clancy. He'd come up behind Logan. There was disapproval in his voice and on his face. "But then maybe the two of you deserve one another, ganging up on Miss Marylin that way."

"She lied and tried to frame me," Rachel seethed, unable to believe that the butler refused to see the truth. Of course Clancy had always had a soft spot for Marylin. But Rachel couldn't help making a last attempt to make him see the truth.

"Otherwise she would have insisted on calling the police."

He gave a humph, dismissing this protest as ridiculous. "She simply didn't want a scandal," he said, then added, "I've called a taxi for you. Mr. Parry would like you to have your things packed and out of here as quickly as possible." Having delivered this message, he turned toward Logan. "Mr. Parry has also suggested that it would be best if you moved to a hotel. I've taken the liberty of having Anne pack your bags." Clancy finished with a curt incline of his head, then turned around in a military fashion and left.

A wave of concern washed over Rachel. Logan had come to her aid. She didn't want to see him harmed either socially or financially. "I'm sorry I got you thrown out," she said with honest remorse.

"I've been thrown out of fancier places than this," he replied with an indifferent shrug.

She breathed a silent sigh of relief. Obviously being tossed out of Justin's home didn't bother him.

He regarded her levelly. "What about the job?"

Rachel again looked around the room. She had no place to go. "Sure. Why not?"

Chapter Three

Why not? The question repeated itself in Rachel's mind as she fought a surge of panic. The moment she had agreed to accompany him, Logan had left her and made plane reservations. Now, just a little more than four hours later, she was seated beside him in the first-class section of a jet awaiting takeoff. All of her worldly belongings had been hastily packed into the two suitcases and steamer trunk now housed in the baggage compartment.

I'll tell you why not, came the terse answer. *You know nothing about this man.* True, he had come to her aid and kept her out of jail, she reminded herself. But that didn't make him a Boy Scout, her argumentative side rebutted.

Logan interrupted her internal debate. "Are you all right?" he asked.

Rachel turned toward her companion. He was watching her worriedly. "I'm fine," she assured him. But she didn't feel fine. A part of her wanted to reach out and trace the line of his jaw with the tip of her finger just to test the texture of his skin, while another part wanted to leap from her seat and race off the plane.

"You're looking a little pale," he persisted. "Are you afraid of flying?"

"No." Meeting his gaze, she heard herself admit, "I'm having second thoughts about the wisdom of accepting your job offer."

A cynical smile tilted one corner of his mouth. "Already missing the crowds and bright lights?"

"No." She hesitated, then her jaw tensed with purpose. Ignoring the doubts plaguing her was stupid. Now, while the door of the plane was still open, was the time to get them out in the open. "I just want to make certain we both understand what my job entails. I'm coming to your farm or ranch or whatever it is to be your housekeeper, and nothing more."

He frowned impatiently at her implication. "You have my word. I'm not luring you out there to attack you." As if her notion was absurd and deserved no more attention, he turned away from her and began reading the magazine he'd brought on board.

For a moment, Rachel scowled at his taut profile, then turned her gaze to the window. He'd given her the assurance she'd asked for. She should be pleased. *And I am,* she told herself. He didn't have to act as if she had no feminine appeal at all, though.

"And—" Logan's cool voice again interrupted her thoughts "—if at any time you want to leave, all you have to do is say so."

She glanced at him, but he had already returned his attention to the article he was reading.

So, what's your problem? she chided herself. They both agreed on why she was going with him and she could leave if it didn't work out. Relax and enjoy the trip, she ordered herself.

But relaxing around Logan James wasn't easy. She found herself studying him covertly. He was obviously very sure of himself, a man who would bend to no other man—or woman, she added, recalling the disgust in his voice when he'd spoken of Justin's allowing himself to be manipulated by his granddaughter.

Logan suddenly turned to face her. "Was there something else you wanted to ask me or tell me?" he demanded in an agitated tone, as if he had sensed her attention and found it irritating.

She'd been caught. Trying to appear as if her interest had been merely due to boredom, she said casually, "I was just wondering how you got that scar."

"I had a small disagreement with some barbed wire I was stringing for a fence," he replied.

Rachel cringed at the thought of the pain he must have experienced. "I'd say it looks more like a large disagreement."

He shrugged. "A large disagreement would have meant the loss of an eye or a broken limb."

Rachel regarded him dryly. "I get it. And a really major disagreement would have meant a broken neck."

"Something like that," he confirmed. "If the scar bothers you, we can switch seats."

Rachel saw the almost indiscernible tightening of his jaw as he made this offer. Apparently he was self-conscious about his appearance. The discovery took her by surprise. He seemed so confident, so certain of himself. Now it was her turn to feel disconcerted. It had been rude of her to mention his scar. "It doesn't bother me. Actually it adds a rather interesting quality to your appearance." She scowled at herself for this last admission. She'd meant to stop with a simple assurance that she didn't find the scar disturbing. She hoped he wouldn't think she was trying to flirt with him. That would mean setting the ground rules again.

But his only response was a nod. Then he turned back to his magazine.

Obviously she had been mistaken about the extent of his self-consciousness, she decided. It was equally obvious that her opinion of him meant nothing to him. He was just being polite when he offered to switch seats. She reminded herself that in his eyes she was only the hired help. And that suited her just fine. She'd learned early in life that impersonal relationships were the safest, and just this morning Justin Parry had once again provided her with proof of that.

If you don't expect friendship or loyalty, then you can't be hurt when you don't get it, she reminded herself. She wouldn't forget that fact again.

By the time they reached Billings, Montana, Rachel's muscles were stiff and she was tired. It had been a long flight with a layover in Salt Lake City. But it was anxiety and tension that had really worn her down. She'd tried to relax but found she couldn't. A part of her was having trouble believing she'd agreed to be a housekeeper for an almost total stranger in the middle of nowhere.

During one of their brief moments of conversation, Logan had informed her that Hank Thompson, his foreman, would be meeting them. He'd also told her that his current housekeeper, the one who was pregnant, was Hank's wife, Wanda.

As they disembarked, Rachel scanned the group of people waiting to greet the passengers. A tall, lanky cowboy, standing a couple of inches over six feet in his boots, waved when he spotted Logan. So this was Hank. He was younger than she'd expected. She placed him in his late twenties. Like

Logan, he had dark hair and brown eyes. His features, however, were softer than Logan's, giving him a less intimidating air. Rachel saw surprise register on his face when he realized she was the one with Logan.

A grin of masculine approval replaced the look of surprise as quick introductions were made. "When Logan told us he'd found someone to help Wanda around the house and take over when she has the baby," he said, his grin broadening, "Wanda and I expected someone a little more matronly."

Logan's smile didn't reach his eyes. "Keep in mind that you're a married man," he warned.

Hank laughed. "No way I'd forget that. When you've got a redheaded wife, forgetfulness like that can be right dangerous."

The sudden gleam in his eyes at the mention of his wife was proof to Rachel that here was a man who loved the woman he was married to.

"Wanda's going to be real happy to have another woman to talk to," Hank said, returning his attention to Rachel. A teasing note entered his voice. "Now tell me, how'd a rough customer like Logan convince you to come out here?"

There was open welcome in his voice and manner, but she couldn't help wondering how long that would last once he found out about her past. Obviously Logan had told him nothing.

"It's been a long day," Logan cut in before Rachel could respond. "Let's get her to the ranch before you talk her to death."

Hank looked mildly taken aback by Logan's commanding tone. Then he shrugged and his good humor returned. "Guess New York can get on anyone's nerves." Removing his hat, he made a sweeping bow toward Rachel. "Welcome to Montana. Now I'll get you home."

As the three started toward the luggage area, Rachel glanced at Logan. So he wasn't all that certain once the truth became known about her being accepted here, either. *By tomorrow he'll probably be regretting he brought me,* she thought. The terse set of his jaw caused her to add, *If he isn't already.*

A helicopter! The cold wind whirled around Rachel as she stood staring at the vehicle that would carry them to their destination.

"Climb in," Logan ordered. "It's cold out here."

His hands were around her waist lifting her inside before Rachel could react. Once in the belly of the machine, she looked around. There were two seats up front. Where she stood was a cargo area.

"Move up," Logan commanded.

She scooted toward the front as he and Hank shoved her trunk inside. It was immediately followed by her suitcases, Logan's luggage, and then Hank and Logan.

"You take the passenger seat," Logan said as he brushed past her and climbed into the pilot's seat. "Hank'll use the jump seat."

Still mildly stunned, Rachel merely nodded and obeyed.

As she eased herself into the seat, she glanced at Logan. His silence while they'd found their luggage and carried it out to the helicopter had convinced her that he was already regretting having brought her here. Any moment now she expected him to announce he'd changed his mind about hiring her. Instead, as she seated herself, he reached across and fastened her seat belt. Then his gloved hand closed around hers. "This machine is perfectly safe," he said reassuringly.

A warmth spread up her arm and she felt herself being drawn into the dark depths of his eyes. A sense of security she had never felt before enveloped her. *There's no security beyond what you build in yourself,* she reminded herself curtly. She jerked her gaze away. "I'll take your word for it," she said stiffly.

Releasing her hand abruptly, Logan turned his attention to the controls.

Rachel hadn't looked at her watch when they took off, so by the time they landed, she wasn't certain how long the flight had been. But she did know that they had traveled over a vast expanse of open, uninhabited land. And she was cold. There was still snow on the ground and the heating system in the helicopter wasn't adequate to keep the chill out of the air.

"Wanda'll have some hot coffee brewing and she's made a real nice dinner complete with apple pie," Hank said encouragingly as he helped her out of the helicopter.

Rachel had gathered from the brief bits of conversation between Logan and Hank at the airport that Hank and Wanda were the only other people at the ranch. And that Wanda was a little more than seven months into her pregnancy.

Logan set the helicopter down about fifty yards from a sprawling ranch house. Because it was already after dark, Rachel could discern only shadowed images of corrals and outbuildings.

"We'll get the steamer trunk tomorrow," Logan said, as he handed the suitcases to Hank. A moment later, he was out of the helicopter. Picking up one of the bags, he fastened his free hand securely around Rachel's arm and began guiding her toward the house. "Be careful. The ground's a little uneven," he warned.

Rachel was immediately aware of the strength in the sinewy fingers that gripped her and helped her negotiate the unfamiliar terrain. The touch stirred an unexpected excitement within her. *That kind of feeling is only going to get you into trouble,* she scolded herself. This man had no interest in her as a woman. She was merely someone to clean and cook for him.

A very pregnant, short, cute redhead with brown eyes met them at the door. "I'm Wanda Thompson," she introduced herself to Rachel as they entered. Like her husband, Wanda revealed a momentary expression of surprise on her face at the sight of Rachel, followed quickly by one of curiosity. But her sense of hospitality won out. "I fixed up the third guest bedroom for her," she said to Logan. Then her face tinted pink with embarrassment. "I thought she'd be needing it," she added dubiously, her gaze shifting between Logan and Rachel. Clearly the thought they might be intending to share a bed had suddenly crossed her mind.

"She will," Logan replied in a firm, businesslike tone. "I'll show her the way while you put dinner on the table."

Wanda nodded. Her cheeks still lightly tinted with embarrassment, she headed for the kitchen.

Silently, Rachel followed Logan through the living room and down a door-lined hallway.

"This house wasn't built with live-in servants in mind, so you don't have separate quarters," he said as he led her down the hall. "You will, however, have your own private bathroom, except when we have company." He nodded at the third door on her left as he spoke to indicate the location of the bathroom. Coming to a halt at the next door, which also happened to be the last door on the left side of the hall, he shoved it fully open with his booted foot and carried her suitcase inside.

Rachel followed him in and let her gaze travel around the room. It had a comfortable, homey air. The walls were light blue, the curtains and bedspread white, and the furniture Early American.

"After you've freshened up, just follow the hall back in the direction we came," Logan directed. "The kitchen's at the opposite end of the house. I'll give you a complete tour after dinner."

Rachel barely got out a thank-you before he was gone. But he didn't go far. She heard a second pair of booted footsteps. Returning to her doorway, she saw Hank set Logan's suitcase down in front of a door just one down from hers on the right-hand side of the hall before he headed on to her room with the other. Logan picked up his suitcase and entered the room.

"Are you going to be needing anything from your trunk?" Hank asked politely as she accepted the piece of luggage from him.

"No," she replied, her gaze shifting back to the room Logan had entered. It had never occurred to her that she would be sharing such close quarters with her employer. *It's no closer than if we lived in the same apartment building,* she reasoned, irritated with herself for being so disconcerted. He was, after all, merely a man—*and* one who had shown no interest in her except as his cook and housekeeper.

"Evenin', then," Hank said, and with a tip of his hat, strode off.

There was a finality in Hank's voice that confused Rachel. She'd thought she would be eating dinner with him and his wife. She was tempted to run after him, but he was already at the end of the hall. *I probably just misinterpreted his tone,* she told herself as she went back into her room.

But when she entered the kitchen a few minutes later she found only Logan there. "I told Wanda we could serve ourselves. She and Hank have gone on home," he said, noticing her glancing around for the others.

"Home?" Rachel stared at him. "I thought they lived here."

"They live in the foreman's house." Logan nodded toward the darkness outside the window. "It's about a hundred yards in that direction. They like their privacy and I like mine." Rachel looked at the rectangular table in the center of the large kitchen. It was set cozily for two. The thought that there was a little too much privacy in this house crossed her mind. Again she chided herself and told herself that she was merely unnerved because she was so tired. Still, she said, "Since I'm the hired help, it would be more proper for me to serve you in the dining room."

He frowned impatiently. "I prefer to eat in the kitchen. Tonight we'll eat together because that's the most practical thing to do. Afterward, if you prefer to eat alone, you may eat when and where you like. Right now, I'm too hungry to debate the point." As he spoke, he picked up an iron pot and carried it to the table. Inside was a beef stew.

Rachel's stomach growled as the aroma wafted toward her. He was right. First they would eat, then she would discuss future arrangements.

"There's corn bread in the oven. It should be done about now," he said. As if adding credence to his words, the timer on the stove began to buzz. In response to his unspoken order, Rachel immediately crossed to the oven.

A few minutes later, they were seated at the table, both eating hungrily. The stew and corn bread were delicious, and the apple pie was the best Rachel had ever tasted. It wasn't until she was eating her last bite that she finally took the time to study her surroundings. Immediately her nervousness returned. Even with her disquieting employer seated nearby, this kitchen was too comfortable. The aroma, the warmth, the ambience of the room—as if it had been lovingly used for generations—all came together to create the atmosphere of the home she'd always longed for, but never had. *This is Logan James's home. For me it is merely a place of short-term employment,* she reminded herself sternly.

"Both Hank and I've been a little worried about Wanda not getting enough rest. She's been looking extra tired lately. So I told her to sleep in tomorrow. I figured you could fix breakfast on your own," Logan said. A dubious quality entered his voice. "You did say you could cook...."

His intonation made this last remark more of a question than a statement. "I worked as a waitress and part-time short-order cook before I got my chauffeur's license," she replied.

A crooked smile tilted one corner of his mouth. "I hope you're not going to tell me that you gave up being a cook because your customers revolted."

His unexpected, boyishly charming smile caught her off guard, and she experienced a warm, pleasurable curling sensation in the pit of her stomach. This was not the kind of reaction she wanted to have toward him. What she wanted was to be as immune to him as he was to her. "No," she replied, keeping her voice cool and impersonal. "I simply preferred being a chauffeur to slaving over a greasy griddle."

The smile disappeared and his manner once again became that of the polite but distant host. "How did you become a chauffeur?"

Rachel had expected him to return to his usual silence. This was the first time since they'd left New York that he'd shown any interest in holding more than a one- or two-word conversation with her. It occurred to her that he might have realized just how little he knew about the stranger he'd invited into his home and he'd decided to remedy that. She couldn't blame him. But she didn't like talking about herself. Even more, the question he'd asked didn't spark good memories. Rachel stared into her coffee cup. "A couple of our regular customers worked for a limousine service. One of them offered to teach me to drive. I took him up on it. I liked the sense of control I had behind the wheel." Despite her attempt to keep her voice emotionless, her fatigue allowed a touch of bitterness to creep in when she mentioned the offer of the lessons. Glancing up, she saw Logan studying her more closely.

"What happened to your chauffeur friend?" he asked.

Rachel smiled cynically. "Turned out he wasn't a friend. He wanted... compensation in return for the lessons. I wasn't willing to provide it. He threatened to get a little violent. I threatened to tell his wife. He backed off and left me alone, and I went to a driving school for the rest of my training." Her jaw tensed as the disillusionment she'd felt again washed over her; she'd thought the man had honestly wanted to be her friend. "But I learned a valuable lesson from the experience," she said, meeting Logan's gaze levelly. "I learned that no one gives anything for nothing. Eventually they'll demand a payment of some kind."

He frowned. "That's a pretty cynical view of life."

"It's a realistic view," she countered with conviction.

For a moment he looked as if he was going to argue with her. But instead he pushed his chair back, rose from the table and carried his dishes to the sink.

Rachel rose, too, and began to look for containers in which to store the leftover food. Hearing water running, she glanced toward the sink and saw Logan rinsing off the dishes and putting them in the dishwasher. It seemed incongruous for him to be doing such a mundane household chore. This wasn't the image she wanted to maintain of him. She wanted to think of him as cool and distant, and a male chauvinist of the highest order. "I can do those," she said, striding toward the sink. "It's my job."

"Officially you don't start work until tomorrow morning," he replied, ignoring her as he started toward the table for more dishes. "Tonight we're both tired. As soon as we've straightened up in here, I'll give you a quick tour, and then I'm going to bed." As an afterthought he added, "I generally eat breakfast around six."

"Six is good," she replied with an outwardly indifferent shrug while inwardly she groaned. She was normally an early riser, but if she was going to get his breakfast ready by six, she'd have to be up an hour earlier, and 5 a.m was still nighttime in her book. *You're on a ranch now,* she reminded herself.

Logan insisted on drying the pots and pans after she'd washed them, and again she experienced an unsettlingly warm curling sensation in the pit of her stomach. Okay, so he was kind of attractive with a dish towel in his hand, but there was nothing personal between them now and there never would be. She gave the counter a final wipe, then breathed a sigh of relief as she laid the cloth on the side of the sink to dry overnight. Now for the tour, followed by an escape into the privacy of her room.

As he'd promised, the tour was short. The large kitchen occupied the full width of the back of the house. In addition to the back door, there was a door that led into a laundry room, one that led into the dining room and one that opened into a corridor. On one side of this corridor was a set of double doors that also opened into the dining room. On the other side of the hall was a den with a television and a pool table. At the end of the corridor was the entrance foyer. Off the foyer, a second set of double doors opened into a spacious living room, which occupied the central portion of the house. The foyer also gave access to the hallway that led to the bedrooms. "My study is the first door on your right," Logan said as they started down this hall. "Next to it is my bedroom and bath."

That took care of that side of the hall, Rachel mused, mentally designating that side of the suddenly narrow-seeming corridor as his private domain. He nodded toward their left. "The first two rooms are more guest bedrooms. That third door is the door to the bathroom that adjoins your room."

That left only her room, the place she most wanted to be right now. As they'd made their quick tour, the house had begun to feel very empty and secluded with only the two of them there. It wasn't that Logan had made any sort of improper advance toward her. In fact, he'd been about as standoffish as anyone could be without being rude. It was her own reactions to him that were causing her to be tense.

He'd turned off the lights as they went through the house. Now he stopped beside his bedroom door. "You can leave the hall light on if you like," he offered. Then adding a quick good-night, he entered his room and closed the door behind him.

A scowl spread across Rachel's face as she continued down the hall and went into her room. She was attracted to him. She'd fought it every inch of the way and she'd tried to deny it from the moment she'd first seen him. But she couldn't lie to herself any longer. *It's just a passing thing,* she told herself. If he hadn't come to her aid at the Parrys', the attraction would probably be gone by now. She was still having a hard time accepting that he'd stood up for her. Of course, as he'd pointed out, he'd done it because it was a matter of honor with him. However, the fact remained that he had put his friendship with Justin, not to mention a half-million-dollar deal, on the line.

He is not attracted to me, though, and this is only a temporary arrangement, she reminded herself curtly. Besides, she was probably just experiencing these peculiar responses to him because she was exhausted. It had been a long day. Once she got a good night's sleep, the crazy reactions she had toward him would disappear.

Chapter Four

When her alarm went off the next morning, Rachel groaned, hit the snooze button and snuggled back under the covers. Vaguely she heard the sound of a horse whinnying. Suddenly both eyes popped open as she remembered where she was and why.

Fully awake now, she tossed the covers aside, turned off the alarm completely, then headed for the bathroom. A few minutes later she was in the kitchen. She'd heard movement in Logan's room when she'd passed his door.

"Coffee, first," she instructed herself.

She had just plugged in the percolator when a knock sounded on the back door followed by Wanda's entrance. "I'm too used to getting up early," the woman said in answer to the look of surprise on Rachel's face. Walking over to the stove, she turned the oven on low and placed the square cake pan she had brought inside. "I made some cinnamon buns. They'll keep warm in there while we finish cooking breakfast. I didn't think it was fair to make you find everything in this kitchen on your own."

Rachel rewarded the woman with a guarded smile. She'd seen the inquisitive expression in Wanda's eyes and guessed that at least fifty percent of the reason Wanda was there was curiosity.

"Do you want to set the table or fry the bacon?" Wanda asked good-naturedly.

"I'll fry," Rachel replied. "I need the practice. Besides I'm not sure where any of the dishes are."

The redhead nodded. Then an embarrassed flush tinted her cheeks. "Shall I set one or two places? With you living here with Logan—" She paused abruptly, then began again, "I mean with the two of you living under the same roof and sharing the same kitchen, I didn't know if you had arranged to eat your meals together or not."

"I think it would be more proper for us to eat apart," Rachel said, letting Wanda know that her relationship with her boss was not personal. "I'll just wait until he's eaten and left, then I'll fix myself some breakfast."

Wanda smiled brightly to cover her embarrassment. "Even though I ate with Hank, I might have a bite with you, too," she said as she began to set the table for one. "The first five months of this pregnancy I couldn't keep hardly anything down. Now I'm hungry all the time."

Rachel forced a smile while she wondered how long Wanda's friendliness would last once the woman learned about her past.

"What did your folks think of your coming all this way?" Wanda asked, as she finished setting the table and checked to make certain there was orange juice. "Or are you originally from this part of the country?"

"I don't have any close family," Rachel replied. In spite of her attempt to keep her tone unemotional, a defensiveness crept into it.

"Oh." Wanda looked mildly disconcerted and again her cheeks reddened. "I'm sorry. I didn't mean to pry. It's just that I hardly ever have anyone to talk to."

For the next couple of minutes a silence hung between the two women. It was an uncomfortable silence. Not wanting to seem unfriendly, Rachel asked conversationally, "How long have you lived here at Mr. James's ranch?"

Wanda smiled brightly again, obviously relieved that the silence had come to an end. "Ever since I married Hank. That was four years ago. My parents insisted that we wait until I was twenty-one. My dad runs a hardware store in Billings. I think my parents were hoping I'd find someone who worked a little closer to home. But Hank's been real good to me and they like him. 'Course, my mother wants me to come live with her for my last month. She wants to be certain I'm near a hospital when it's time for the baby to come. But I don't want to be away from Hank."

Listening to her, Rachel found herself envying the woman. Wanda had people who loved her and a life she could rattle on about without the worry of being rejected.

Wanda was now listing the names of her five brothers and sisters and telling Rachel that her mother and youngest sister were going to visit after the baby was born and help her for the first couple of months. "In fact, if Logan hadn't found you," the woman finished, "Mary, my second oldest sister, was going to come up in a couple of weeks and help me out around here. She just graduated from junior college but hasn't found a job yet. Anyway, she wasn't really looking forward to it. Logan intimidates her and she doesn't like the isolation."

He intimidates me, Rachel admitted mentally. As for the isolation, it was a shock, too. Despite Justin's description, she hadn't expected anything this remote. When Logan had said she could just pick up and leave whenever it suited her, she'd thought she could call a cab. Now she doubted there was a taxi service anywhere within a hundred miles, maybe two hundred. Scooping the bacon out of the frying pan, Rachel noticed that a silence had again fallen over the kitchen. Glancing over her shoulder, she saw Wanda watching her with a pained expression. It was clear the woman's curiosity was getting the better of her.

"I hope you won't think I'm prying again, but where did Logan find you?" Wanda asked, the words coming out as if she simply couldn't contain them any longer.

Rachel drew a shaky breath. Might as well get this over with, she told herself. She lifted the last piece of bacon from the skillet and set it on a paper towel to drain. After turning off the heat under the pan, she faced the pregnant redhead. "I was working as Justin Parry's chauffeur. I was accused of stealing. I have a juvenile record for theft and spent time in an institution for delinquent girls when I was in my teens. However, I hadn't stolen the jewels I was accused of stealing, and Mr. James came to my rescue. I still got fired, and he offered me this job because he said he didn't think he could find anyone else to take it."

"Oh," Wanda responded weakly, a guarded look coming over her face as if she wasn't certain Rachel really *was* innocent and maybe wasn't totally safe to be around.

This was what Rachel had expected. She'd seen this same look a hundred times before. Furious with herself that it still hurt, she cynically wondered if Wanda was now considering shipping all her valuables home to her parents.

"I thought I saw Hank heading toward the barns." Logan's voice broke the heavy stillness that had descended over the room.

Rachel swung around to find him standing in the kitchen doorway. She'd been so nervous facing Wanda she hadn't heard his approach.

"Wanda, would you mind seeing if you can find him and ask him to check on Miss Rita? I'm worried that she might drop her foal early." It was politely spoken, but it was an order.

"Sure thing," Wanda said, clearly relieved to have an excuse to escape.

"How do you want your eggs?" Rachel asked coolly, getting back to her cooking as Wanda pulled on her coat and left.

"I suppose you're best at hard boiling them," Logan replied dryly. In the same dry tone he asked, "Do you always do that?"

She turned to face him, challenge in her eyes. "Do what?"

"Hit people with your past before giving them a chance to even say hello?"

Her back stiffened with defiance. "I didn't see any reason to put it off. I figured Wanda would find out sooner or later. And whether she'd gotten to know me or not, the reaction would be the same—she'd suddenly decide that I wasn't good companion material." To prove her point, she continued coolly, "I'd known a lot of those people at Justin's home for several years. I'd eaten with them, worked with them. I even took care of a couple of them when they were sick. I'd never given any of them a single reason to believe that I wasn't completely reformed. But you, a stranger, were the only one who stood up for me." The challenge in her eyes intensified. "Tell me honestly, if you'd known, before you took your stand, that I'd been in jail, would you still have been so quick to come to my aid?"

For a long moment he regarded her thoughtfully, then he said, "I've always tried to be fair in my dealings with people. Yes, I would still have come to your aid."

She was finding it difficult to continue meeting his gaze. There was a depth in his dark eyes that tantalized her, and she found herself wanting to trust him. But she'd been disappointed too many times in the past. "Then you're a very unusual person," she said, her tone indicating that she was skeptical of his assurance. "So," she tried again, "how do you like your eggs?"

"Maybe you've just been associating with the wrong people," he replied, refusing to be diverted.

"I never would have thought of you as being naive," she countered.

He grinned. "Neither would I. But then we all have our weaknesses."

That he could laugh at himself startled her, but even more astonishing was the infectiousness of his grin. She felt the corners of her mouth tilting up in a smile. A warning signal went off in her brain. She was finding him much too likable. Abruptly she started toward the refrigerator. "You still haven't told me how you want your eggs," she reminded him.

"Do you always do that?"

"Now what have I done?" she demanded. His probing was setting her nerves on a razor's edge.

"Shut people out."

She turned to face him. "It saves me a lot of disappointments." Realizing how open she had been, her jaw tensed, and turning away from him, she jerked open the refrigerator door. "Now, *how* do you want your eggs?"

"Over easy," he replied, moving toward the coffeepot.

Hank and Wanda returned about the time Rachel was placing a plate of eggs in front of Logan.

"They came out more scrambled than 'over easy,'" she was saying. "I'm a little out of practice."

Logan gave an indifferent shrug. "They look fine to me."

But the expression on Hank's face when he saw the plate let Rachel know that she needed a lot more practice. She also noticed that behind the foreman's amicable manner was a guardedness that hadn't been there the night before. Obviously Wanda had told him about Rachel's past, and he, too, was questioning his boss's judgment in bringing her here.

While Hank joined Logan at the table and the two began to discuss what had happened around the ranch during Logan's absence and what chores needed to be taken care of, Wanda poured Hank a cup of coffee and carried it to him. Then turning her attention to Rachel, she said, "I thought we'd bake bread today."

"You'll have to teach me," Rachel replied, relieved that the woman wasn't planning to shun her. As she spoke, she caught a glance from Hank out of the corner of her eye. It suggested that she needed quite a few lessons around the kitchen. There was also a protectiveness when his gaze swung toward his wife. Rachel's stomach knotted. He was worried about leaving Wanda with her. She could read it in his eyes.

For a moment, Rachel considered telling Logan she had changed her mind about the job and asking him to make arrangements for her to get back to Billings as quickly as possible. But the words refused to come. Philosophically she reminded herself that she'd always had to prove herself wherever she'd gone. It would be naive of her to think Logan's ranch would be any different.

Wanda had begun explaining how to make bread. Focusing her attention on the redhead, Rachel also assured herself that her staying had nothing to do with Logan himself. She was staying because this ranch was a change from the city, and a change was what she wanted at the moment.

A few minutes later, when the men rose to leave, she noticed Hank hesitate. "You going to be all right, honey?" he asked Wanda.

"I'm going to be just fine," she assured him as she began to knead the dough she had just shown Rachel how to mix.

"You ring the bell if you need me," he instructed, following Logan toward the door at a slow pace.

"I will," Wanda replied, rewarding him with an impatient grimace.

Logan was already out the door and heading toward the barns. Giving his wife a final glance, Hank hurried after him.

Rachel's nerves were near the breaking point. It bothered her that Hank was worried about leaving his wife in her company. And she couldn't help wondering if, beneath her confident surface, Wanda wasn't a little scared herself. *You should be used to reactions like this by now,* she chided mentally and ordered herself to ignore it. But she didn't like making Wanda uncomfortable. After all, the woman was pregnant. As the door closed behind the two men, she said stiffly, "You really are safe with me."

Wanda gave a shrug as if to deny she'd been worried. But she couldn't entirely hide the cautious edge in her voice as she said, "You have to excuse Hank. He's always been overly protective of me, and since I've been pregnant, he's gotten even worse.''

Rachel felt a jab of envy in the pit of her stomach. "You're lucky to have someone who cares so much," she said with sincerity.

Wanda paused to study Rachel. "I am," she confirmed. Once again curiosity was strong in her eyes. "You said you have no family?"

"None I'm close to," Rachel replied, keeping her gaze focused on the woman's hands as Wanda kneaded the dough in a rhythmic fashion. Unexpectedly the thought of Logan feeling as protective toward her as Hank felt toward Wanda came into her mind and caused a surge of warmth to wash through her. *This rarefied air is affecting my brain,* she decided.

A small gasp from Wanda caused her to look up. She saw a look of pain flash across the woman's face. "Are you all right?" she asked nervously.

Wanda had paused in her kneading to take several short, panting breaths. "The baby just kicked a little harder than usual," she replied when she was able to get her breathing back to normal.

But Rachel didn't like the sudden paleness of Wanda's skin. "How about letting me finish the kneading and you sit down for a while," she suggested.

Wanda nodded. Resting a hand on her stomach as if to soothe the child inside, she eased into a nearby chair.

During the remainder of the morning, Rachel insisted on doing all of the work around the house with Wanda acting only as a supervisor.

"We'll reheat the leftover stew and have fresh-baked bread for the men when they come for lunch," Wanda instructed as Rachel straightened Logan's bathroom. "Lunchtime we generally all eat together. Makes it easier for me."

A mild hint of Logan's after-shave still lingered and it was having an unnervingly tantalizing effect on Rachel's senses. "Should we be doing something with that bread dough, then?" she asked, looking for any excuse to escape this room.

Wanda glanced at her watch. "Yes," she replied, and started back toward the kitchen.

Rachel caught the edge of relief in the redhead's voice. Although Wanda had been pleasant and for the most part outwardly relaxed during the morning, Rachel had continued to sense an underlying guardedness about her. Well, at least she didn't insist on locking away the family silver and keeping the key, Rachel mused.

During the meal, the men discussed the site of the new corral they were planning, and Wanda and Rachel decided on a dinner menu for Logan.

Rachel noticed that Hank seemed more relaxed toward her now, not totally at ease, but less suspicious. However, it wasn't Hank who garnered her greatest attention. It was Wanda. The redhead grimaced covertly several times during the meal as if the baby was kicking exceptionally hard. The womanly protectiveness she'd felt earlier in the day toward Wanda grew stronger. When the meal ended and she and Wanda rose to clear the table, she said, "I can take care of cleaning up these dishes, and it seems to me we've gotten the house into shape for today. I thought I'd spend the afternoon unpacking, and I'm sure I can fix the dinner you've planned for tonight. Why don't you take the remainder of the day off and rest?

"Maybe I will," Wanda agreed without argument. "Carrying around this extra weight is a bit tiring."

Hank and Logan had been on their way out the door. Abruptly Hank stopped and turned back toward his wife. "I'll walk you home."

Logan had stopped, too. He watched as Hank helped Wanda with her coat, then holding the door open for them, he said to Hank, "I'll meet you at the corral in a few minutes."

Rachel busied herself with clearing the table. She'd expected Logan to continue on down to the corral, but instead he returned to the table, picked up a plate and cup and carried them to the sink.

"Looks like you and Wanda got along all right," he said as he set the dishes on the counter and started back toward the table.

"Good enough," she replied, adding dryly, "And it seems that you've halfway convinced Hank that I'm not too dangerous to leave in his wife's company."

An expression of apology came over Logan's features. "I'm sorry about Hank's attitude. He's really protective of Wanda."

"I think it's nice that he cares so much," she said honestly. Again she found herself wondering what it would be like to have Logan feel that way toward her. *Don't be an idiot,* she chided herself. *He's your boss and nothing more.* But it wasn't easy keeping the wall of distinction between them when he was carrying dishes to the sink and scraping them. "I can clean up in here by myself," she said stiffly. "It's my job."

He rewarded the dismissal in her voice with an impatient scowl. Then his expression became unreadable and, giving a shrug, he set aside the plate that he'd just picked up and left the room.

When he passed back through the kitchen a few minutes later on his way out, he paused to inform her that he liked to have his dinner around six. His manner was cool and businesslike.

"And that's how I want it," she informed the emptiness surrounding her. But standing at the kitchen sink, she could see him through the window as he walked toward the barns. He moved lithely and she felt a curious weakening in her limbs at the sight. Frustrated by her body's continued disturbing reactions to him, she jerked her gaze away from the view and concentrated on the dishes.

It was midafternoon when Rachel finished unpacking. For the first time since her arrival, she had nothing to do for the next couple of hours. Wandering through the large, empty house, she expected a feeling of loneliness to descend upon her, but it didn't.

However, a nagging concern about Wanda did persist, and she couldn't stop herself from going to check on her.

Walking along the gravel path between the large house and the smaller one, Rachel let her gaze travel in a sweeping circle. The sky was clearer than any sky she'd ever seen and the air smelled of horses and earth. It was so different here from any place she'd ever known. But instead of feeling uneasy, a sense of peace—as if she'd found where she belonged—came over her. "You don't belong here," she said aloud to herself. "This is merely a temporary job."

Uncertain of her welcome, Rachel made no move to try to enter the house when Wanda answered her knock. "I just thought I'd drop by for a moment and see how you were feeling," she said, remaining on the porch with the screened door between them.

"I'm doing just fine," Wanda replied, obviously surprised to find Logan's new housekeeper on her stoop. "Have you run into some trouble finding what you need for dinner?"

"No." Rachel forced a smile. The woman wasn't going to invite her in. She was used to not always being welcome, but for some reason the lack of acceptance this time hurt more than usual. "I just wanted to get some fresh air and thought I'd make certain the baby wasn't giving you any unexpected trouble," she said, beginning to ease her way off the porch. "See you tomorrow."

"Wait." Wanda frowned as if angry with herself. Then she smiled sheepishly. "I was making myself some hot chocolate. Would you like some?" She opened the door to add encouragement to her invitation.

Pride almost caused Rachel to refuse. She wasn't certain if Wanda honestly wanted her inside or if the woman's natural hospitality had forced the invitation. But there was only one way to find out, she told herself. Besides, life here would be a lot more pleasant if she could convince Wanda that there was nothing to fear from her company. "Sure," she replied, changing direction and moving back toward the door.

Once she was inside the cozy two-bedroom house, Wanda said, "Have a seat," and she nodded toward the small kitchen table by the window.

As Rachel obeyed, the redhead moved toward the stove. For a long moment a silence filled the room, then Wanda turned toward her guest. "I know Hank and I have been kind of standoffish. We're so used to being alone up here it takes time for us to adjust to someone new."

"Especially someone with a police record," Rachel added, deciding that if they could get it all out in the open, then maybe she could dispel Wanda and Hank's remaining concern.

Wanda frowned thoughtfully. "Yes," she admitted. "But Hank says that Logan says you had good reason for what you did." She smiled crookedly. "And if only half the stories I've heard tell about them are true, Hank and Logan weren't such angels themselves in their younger days."

Rachel had a tremendous urge to ask Wanda to tell her about Logan's younger days but she bit back the words. She didn't want to appear overly interested in her boss. *Because I'm not,* she assured herself. "Well, I've learned my lesson," she said instead.

Wanda gave her an encouraging smile. "Logan obviously believes that or he wouldn't have brought you here. And I'm willing to accept Logan's judgment. He's a cautious man."

"I'm surprised he never married," Rachel said, then was shocked at herself. It was definitely prying and she'd just promised herself that she wouldn't.

"He was engaged once," Wanda replied as she added more milk and chocolate to the mixture on the stove. "I never met her. That was before Hank and I got married. Anyway, according to Hank, it was someone Logan met in college. He brought her up here a couple of times." As if a point of modesty needed to be made, she inserted quickly, "That was when his father was still alive, so it wasn't as if they weren't chaperoned." Then she continued conversationally, "But the girl didn't like the isolation. When she discovered that Logan was dead set on living here, she broke off the engagement. Hank says she married a doctor and moved to St. Louis."

That Logan had once been engaged bothered Rachel more than she wanted to admit. She recalled the look on his face when he'd accused Justin of allowing himself to be manipulated by a woman. At the time she'd thought it was merely arrogance. Now she wondered if it was because he was still in love with the woman who had left him. *His love life is none of my concern,* she told herself firmly. But she couldn't entirely control her curiosity about her employer. "You said his father was still alive then, but you didn't mention his mother. Did he lose her at a young age?"

Wanda grinned as she seated herself. "Oh, no. She's still alive and kicking." Her grin turned into a thoughtful frown. "She just couldn't stand the isolation up here, either. She stayed for five years, then left and divorced Logan's father. She married a lawyer from Los Angeles by the name of Mc-Greggor, and has three sons and a daughter by him. Logan lived with her until he was fourteen. By then it was clear he was cut from the same cloth as his father. He'd been spending all his summers here and he and his dad had stayed real close. His mother finally agreed to let him come back here and live with his dad permanently. 'Course he still keeps close ties to his mom and stepfather and his half brothers and sister. Family means a lot to him."

Rachel stared into her cup of hot chocolate. Family—the kind whose members cared about one another—was something she'd never had. "It must be nice to have people who care about you," she thought, then flushed when she realized she'd spoken aloud.

Wanda was studying her, sympathy mingled with interest in her eyes. "I can't imagine not having some family. It must be difficult."

Pity was something Rachel had never been able to abide. A mask of indifference came over her features. "It has its advantages. For instance, I don't have anyone trying to tell me how to lead my life."

"I suppose," Wanda replied without conviction.

Not wanting to allow the other woman more opportunity to ask personal questions, Rachel said quickly, "Have you chosen names for your baby?" To her relief, Wanda happily launched into a detailed recitation of how difficult it was to make a decision.

For the next hour the women talked about babies. Actually Wanda talked and Rachel listened. But Rachel didn't mind. In a way, it was almost frightening how much she wanted to belong here. *Dangerous* would be a better word, she thought as she left Wanda's home and walked back to Logan's. She'd let herself start to believe she had a place in Justin's home and she'd been disappointed. She had no intention of giving in to that kind of weakness again. "Think 'temporary employee,'" she ordered herself as she entered Logan's kitchen.

"I know the isolation up here can get to a person." Logan's voice startled her as she began unbuttoning her coat. "But I didn't expect to hear you talking to yourself already."

She saw him standing by the counter pouring himself a cup of freshly brewed coffee. "I'm sorry. I should have been here to fix that for you," she said, embarrassed to have already failed to do her job properly.

"I don't expect to be waited on hand and foot."
He was watching her closely. "Couldn't make out
what you were saying, but that muttering didn't
sound particularly joyous. Are you and Wanda
having trouble getting along?"

If they were, Rachel could easily guess which one
of them would be leaving. "No, we're getting along
just fine," she replied.

He looked relieved. "Glad to hear that," he said
over his shoulder as he headed for the door leading
into the living room.

For a brief moment, Rachel found herself wish-
ing he was glad because he wanted her there. *He's
glad because he doesn't want to be worried about
who's going to cook and clean up after him for the
next few months,* she quickly reminded herself.

At the door, he paused and turned back. "Been
thinking that when it's only the two of us, it'd be
more practical if you ate with me instead of waiting on me and then eating when I was gone. That
way you wouldn't have to eat cold or dried-out
food." It was more of an order than a suggestion.

A protest rose in Rachel's throat. She preferred
to keep a distance between herself and this cowboy. But before she could respond, he left.

"You're living under the same roof with him,"
she muttered as she turned on the oven and washed
the potatoes she was going to bake. "What difference can sitting at the same table with him make?"

A lot of difference was the answer, and it came a little more than an hour later. Still uncertain about her cooking, she'd made certain that she and Wanda had chosen a simple menu—baked potatoes, salad and broiled steak. There was also the fresh-baked bread she and Wanda had made that morning and leftover apple pie.

"Looks good," Logan said as he seated himself.

"Wanda and I chose something for me to make that would be difficult to ruin," she replied honestly as she sat down.

As they started to eat, a tense silence fell over the table. Rachel had spent the past hour telling herself that Logan James was just a man like any other man. But she knew that was a lie the moment he walked through the door. His presence seemed to fill the room. Dressed in his jeans and blue plaid flannel shirt, with his dark hair still slightly damp from his shower and the ends curling just a bit at his neck, she found him incredibly appealing.

Logan had eaten a couple of bites when he put his fork aside and his gaze leveled on her. "Are you going to stay?"

A little voice inside suggested it would be safer to leave, but she heard herself saying, "Yes." She wanted to stay here more than she wanted to admit. But she didn't want Logan guessing that, so she added, "It's better than some of the other jobs I've had."

His expression remained coolly businesslike. "Wanda and Hank will be glad to hear that."

Rachel felt a tingling of disappointment. Logan didn't care whether she stayed or left except for Wanda and Hank's sakes. He's not supposed to care and *you're* not supposed to care if he cares, she berated herself.

"You'll let me know if the isolation gets to you," he continued in the same indifferent tones. "I'd like to have some notice rather than come home one day and find you packed and waiting in the hall."

Rachel studied him. Two women he had loved had done just that, but there was no anger, no emotion of any kind in his manner. There was only acceptance as if this was what he expected to happen. "I'll let you know," she replied.

He nodded, then returned his attention to the meal.

It wasn't until she was serving the dessert that he spoke again. "I figured one more day of Wanda's help is about all you'll need," he said. "I know she's anxious to have her days to herself to get ready for the baby, and Hank wants her to take it easy."

One more day and it would be just the two of them. Rachel felt a sudden wave of nervousness. Hank and Wanda are only a few yards away, she reminded herself.

They might as well be a hundred miles away, she decided a little later as she cleaned up after the meal. In this house in the middle of this vast wilderness, it was as if she and Logan were the only two people in the world. "You're being ridiculous," she admonished herself under her breath.

But as she finished washing the last pan, the thought of the evening ahead caused her back muscles to tighten painfully. Logan had given her free access to the house. "Just behave as if it's your home," he'd told her.

But she didn't want to run into him. The reaction she was having toward him unnerved her too much. She also didn't want to cloister herself in her room.

Cookies! The word popped into her mind like a flash of salvation. Wanda had pointed out a shelf in the pantry filled with cookbooks and boxes containing recipes collected by Logan's grandmother. A few minutes later Rachel had chosen a recipe from one of the books and was gathering the ingredients. Forty-five minutes later she was taking her first batch of freshly baked cookies from the oven.

"Smells like oatmeal cookies in here," Logan said, entering the kitchen. He looked somewhat stunned to find her baking, as if, even though he had hired her as a domestic, he didn't really expect her to act like one.

"I hope you like them, because there's going to be quite a few," she said, suddenly realizing she had no idea what kind of cookies he preferred.

"Oatmeal has always been one of my favorites," he replied, leaning against the counter and watching her as she spooned more batter onto the baking sheet.

In spite of the relaxing effect making cookies had always had on her, his presence was causing her muscles to tense once again. "I didn't know if you liked raisins in your cookies, so I'm baking the first batches without. However, I thought I would add some to the last couple of dozen. I like them."

"Either way is fine with me." For a long moment he continued to study her in silence. But as she slid the second batch into the oven, he admitted what she'd already read on his face. "Truth is I'm a little surprised to find you baking."

The spicy aroma filling the kitchen brought a flood of memories. "My father died when I was five. After that I spent a lot of time at my Grandma Hadley's home. She was always baking cookies." A wistful smile spread across her face. "Her kitchen smelled so good." Suddenly realizing she had been talking about herself, her jaw tensed. She shrugged as if what she'd said had little importance. "Anyway, I just thought I'd bake a few to pass the time. I wanted to see if I remembered how."

He regarded her thoughtfully. "Where is your grandmother now?"

A lump formed in Rachel's throat. She swallowed it back. "She died when I was twelve," she replied.

"I'm sorry," he said with sympathy.

The lump returned to Rachel's throat. She never talked about her grandmother. But Logan made her uneasy, and the smell of baking was having a weakening effect on her. "So was I. She was one of the few bright spots in my childhood."

"I take it that your mother didn't bake too many cookies," he said as he approached the table. Picking up one of the cookies from the cooling rack, he bit into it.

A cynical expression etched itself into Rachel's features. "My mother didn't like cooking at all." Not wanting him to see the pain talking about her family caused, she turned away from him and began gathering the equipment she had used to mix the batter. A bitter memory suddenly flashed into her mind. "I tried baking cookies on my own once, but she got furious at me for messing up her kitchen." Her hand tightened on the beater she was holding. She couldn't believe she was making these confessions. They were things she had kept stored inside and never told anyone.

Logan rounded the table and blocked her retreat to the sink. Capturing her chin in his hand, he forced her to look up at him. "You can mess up my kitchen any time you please," he said in an easy drawl.

His touch sent currents of heat racing through her. But even more distracting was the way she felt herself being drawn into the dark depths of his eyes. A weakness spread through her legs and her heart began to beat more rapidly. She wanted him to kiss her. *No, you don't,* a small voice of sanity warned. *You'd be nothing more to him than a warm body to ease some of the boredom of living alone out here.* When she finally entered a relationship with a man it was going to be based on something more than mere physical attraction. "Thanks," she said stiffly, taking a step back.

Releasing his hold on her, he looked mildly angry with himself as if just then realizing he'd been touching her. The polite, reserved expression returned to his face. "You're welcome," he replied, and after picking up a couple more cookies, he strode out of the kitchen.

The timer on the stove buzzed. Hurrying to remove the latest batch from the oven before they burned, Rachel noticed that her hands were shaking and she scowled angrily. She couldn't believe she was silly enough to let that cowboy affect her so strongly. She obviously didn't have any real effect on him. He'd actually looked relieved to escape from the kitchen. And I'm glad he's gone, she assured herself.

In the back of her mind, though, she couldn't help feeling pleased that he'd taken a couple more cookies.

Chapter Five

During the next few days, Rachel worked out a routine around Logan's schedule. With only him to take care of, her time was flexible and the job wasn't very demanding. After Rachel's second day at the ranch, Wanda had been officially relieved of duties in Logan's home so that she could rest and spend some time fixing up the nursery for her baby.

When Logan had come in for lunch the following day, he'd asked Rachel to check on Wanda occasionally. "She's been having some false labor and Hank's nervous," he'd said.

Rachel hadn't been all that certain Wanda wanted her to drop by, but she'd been planning to take a walk and stop by to check on the woman, anyway. The men's anxiousness had rubbed off on

Rachel. And no matter what Wanda thought of her, Rachel didn't want anything bad to happen to the other woman or her baby.

She'd planned on merely exchanging a few words on the porch, but Wanda had insisted she come in. When she'd prepared to leave, Wanda had said, "I really enjoy the company. We should do this daily."

Rachel guessed that the invitation had been issued more as an attempt to battle boredom than as an offer of friendship. Although the redhead was more relaxed in her company, Rachel still sensed an underlying reservedness. Trust was something everyone had to earn, she'd philosophized. Her past just caused her to have to work harder at it. How much she wanted Wanda and Hank to like and trust her surprised Rachel. Normally she kept her cynical shell intact and declared she didn't care what others thought of her. Then Logan's image entered her mind and she scowled. She refused to admit that he had anything to do with her wanting to be accepted here. However, the midafternoon hot-chocolate breaks with Wanda were now a daily part of her schedule.

Today she was baking apple-filled coffee cakes, one of which she planned to take over to Wanda's. Cooking, she'd decided, was like riding a bicycle—once you learned how, you never really forgot. In fact, she'd discovered she enjoyed it very much.

The sound of a car engine caught her attention as she placed the cakes in the oven. Logan had men-

tioned that he was expecting the vet to come by to
check on Miss Rita's pregnancy, but she was certain he'd said the man would be coming on Friday
and this was only Thursday.

She heard the engine shut off and a car door
open and close. Striding through the house, she
reached the front hall as a knock sounded on the
door.

Rachel answered it and found herself facing a
woman she judged to be in her early fifties. The
visitor's ebony hair was peppered with gray and cut
in a short, sporty style. She was trim and pretty,
and nearly as tall as Rachel. Her expensive tailored
traveling suit added even more to her air of ele-
gance. "I'm Gail McGreggor," the woman introduced herself with a smile that did not reach her
eyes.

Rachel met her gaze. There was no hostility in the
way this visitor was looking at her. There was,
however, some constraint as if she was not certain
what to think of the younger woman in front of her
and was withholding judgment. McGreggor. The
name rung a bell in Rachel's mind. But it was the
woman's brown eyes that held her interest. They
were familiar. Suddenly she remembered that it had
been Wanda who had mentioned the name Mc-
Greggor. This was Logan's mother! "Mrs. Mc-
Greggor," she said with stiff formality, "please
come in."

"Is Logan home?" the woman asked as she entered. "I had the sudden urge to visit him. I hope this won't be an inconvenience."

"No, of course not," Rachel replied quickly. Not wanting Mrs. McGreggor to get the wrong idea about her presence in Logan's home, Rachel continued in polite but cool tones, "I'm Rachel Hadley, Mr. James's new housekeeper."

The older woman made a quick inspection of Rachel, from her pullover sweater to her jeans and sneakers and then back to her face. "I knew he was looking for someone to take over for Wanda," she said, giving no indication of whether she approved or disapproved of her son's choice.

But I'm not what you expected, Rachel added mentally, her gut instinct warning her that Mrs. McGreggor had reservations about her. Rachel's stomach tightened as she wondered if this woman's disapproval would cost her her job. *It might be for the best,* she reasoned. In spite of how hard she'd tried to ignore Logan's appeal, she was constantly aware of him. When he was in the house, she always knew where he was, and when he was out, she found herself wondering where he was and what he was doing. Periodically she'd recall the scar on his cheek, and a chill would shake her as she wondered if he was safe. "I'll ring the bell for him," she said, starting toward the kitchen. "I believe he was planning to be working in the barns this afternoon."

Gail McGreggor placed her hand on Rachel's arm. "There's no need to disturb him. I'm planning to stay a couple of days. I'll see him when he comes in."

"Then you must have luggage," Rachel said, adopting her most polished servant's manner. "I'll bring it in and prepare a room for you."

"My bag is in the trunk," Gail replied, handing Rachel the key to the rented car parked outside. "Thank you," she added as Rachel started toward the door.

The curious edge in Gail McGreggor's voice caused Rachel to glance back. She had the feeling she'd been entirely forgotten as the older woman's gaze traveled slowly around the entrance hall. A nervousness suddenly showed in Gail McGreggor's eyes. "Clay's been dead nearly ten years now and yet I can still feel his presence inside these walls," she said barely above a whisper. Then she walked into the living room.

Logan and his father must have been a great deal alike, Rachel decided as she went out to the car. When she returned to the house with the suitcase, it occurred to her that Gail McGreggor might prefer one guest room over the other. Going in search of the woman, she found the living room empty. The sound of the back door opening caught her attention and she turned toward the kitchen.

"Mother?" she heard Logan saying in surprised tones. "I thought you were the vet coming a day early."

"I hope you don't mind," Gail replied, the uncertainty of her welcome evident in her voice. "I suddenly had the urge to come for a short visit."

"You're always welcome here," Logan assured her with gruff tenderness.

Rachel opened the kitchen door as Gail moved toward her son.

"I'm never sure. I can feel your father's presence as if he was still here, and I wonder if he resents my having left," Gail said as she reached her son and gave him a hug.

"Dad never believed in holding a person against their will," Logan replied, returning her hug. "He accepted your decision."

"I did love him." Gail released her son and took a step back. "But not enough to bear the loneliness of this place."

Rachel found it difficult to think of this house as being a place of loneliness. *It's impolite to eavesdrop,* she admonished herself. Coughing gently, she let them know of her presence. "I was wondering if you had a guest room you prefer?" she said as Mrs. McGreggor turned toward her.

"You can put her in the second one," Logan said before his mother had a chance to answer. His voice and manner were brusque, leaving no doubt that Rachel was his housekeeper and nothing more.

Rachel could have sworn she caught a glimpse of relief in Mrs. McGreggor's eyes. Clearly she didn't measure up to the woman's idea of daughter-in-law material. She felt slightly insulted. *Well, I wasn't planning on being her daughter-in-law, anyway,* Rachel reminded herself. Quickly leaving the kitchen, she went back into the hall, picked up the suitcase and carried it to the guest bedroom. She had just finished making the bed when Gail Mc-Greggor appeared at the door.

"The timer on the stove just buzzed," the woman said. "I thought I'd better come get you."

"Thanks," Rachel replied, and headed instantly for the kitchen. She'd completely forgotten about the cakes. To her relief they were done but not burned. Removing them from the oven, she set them out to cool, then hurried back to the guest room.

"I'll unpack those for you," she offered, finding Mrs. McGreggor removing the contents from the luggage.

"I'm just about done," the woman replied with polite dismissal. "I'll finish."

Rachel would have been happy to leave, but she thought she'd better warn Mrs. McGreggor about the bathroom first so there wouldn't be any embarrassment later. "I'm afraid we're going to be sharing a bathroom," she said apologetically, then added, again in her best deferential voice, "I'll put out clean towels in case you want to wash up."

Mrs. McGreggor nodded. "I'd like to."

Although still anxious to escape, Rachel again hesitated at the door. She was going to have to skip her afternoon break with Wanda, but that didn't mean she couldn't take one of the cakes to her. "When I'm finished in the bathroom, I thought I'd take one of those cakes to Wanda. I'll only be gone a short while."

Mrs. McGreggor gave a shrug of indifference. "There's no need to hurry. It's been a long trip and I plan to take a nap before dinner." Again her gaze traveled around as if she expected to see ghosts emerge from the walls. "She could probably use a bit of company for a while. I had forgotten how desolate this place was."

Isolated, maybe, but not desolate, Rachel thought as she exited the room.

"I noticed you have a guest," Wanda said to Rachel by way of greeting. She was at the door even before Rachel had a chance to knock.

Rachel nodded. "Mrs. McGreggor."

"Well, at least you won't have to worry about her staying too long," Wanda said as she started toward the stove to pour their hot chocolate.

"So I gathered," Rachel replied, hunting plates for their cake.

Seating herself at the table, Wanda looked out her window toward the main house and frowned speculatively. "I wonder why she's here. Normally she only shows up on Logan's birthday. Any other time she wants to see him, she usually calls and cajoles him into coming to Los Angeles for a few days.''

Rachel experienced a surge of concern for Logan. Had his mother come to tell him some distressing news she didn't feel she could deliver over the phone? The thought shook Rachel and she found herself wanting to be there to comfort him if he should need it. But even if he did need comforting, he wouldn't be looking to her for it. Determinedly she turned the conversation to Wanda's baby.

When she returned to the house a little while later, Rachel found Gail McGreggor in the kitchen.

''I was just boiling some water for tea,'' the woman said as she stood by the stove.

There was a tenseness in the woman's manner that rekindled the concern Rachel had felt for Logan a little while earlier. More than ever she was certain Gail McGreggor had come here with a purpose in mind. Suddenly remembering her position in the household, Rachel said quickly, ''I should be doing that. Why don't you make yourself comfortable in the living room or den and I'll bring your tea to you. Or would you rather I bring it to your bedroom?''

Mrs. McGreggor gave a shrug of indifference. ''The living room will be fine.'' She started toward the door, then stopped and turned back. For a moment, she regarded Rachel in silence, then said, "I hope my arrival hasn't caused any problem with your dinner menu."

Rachel had the impression the woman had meant to say something else but had changed her mind. "It's only a problem if you hate pot roast," she replied.

"Pot roast is fine," Mrs. McGreggor said, again moving toward the door.

Behind her, Rachel heard the door open and then close as she got down a tray to place the tea things on. She was trying to decide how many cookies to put on a plate to accompany the tea when Gail McGreggor walked back into the kitchen.

The woman came to a halt a few feet from Rachel and stood facing her levelly. "I'm not good at pretense," she said grimly. "Are you really a jewel thief?"

Rachel's stomach knotted. "No."

Gail McGreggor continued to regard her narrowly. "I got a phone call from Marylin Jennings, Justin Parry's granddaughter. She called on some silly pretext of wanting to know someone's phone number she'd lost. Anyway, during the conversation she mentioned that Logan had become enamored of her grandfather's chauffeur and had brought her out here to his ranch as his housekeeper. She insinuated that the woman was a jewel thief, or at least someone who couldn't be trusted. She said something about a prison record.''

Rachel's shoulders straightened with pride. ''I was Justin Parry's chauffeur. Your son is not enamored of me. He did hire me as his housekeeper. I do have a juvenile jail record. However, I did not steal any jewels.''

''Marylin's current boyfriend made a pass at Rachel. Marylin found out and to get even attempted to frame Rachel for a jewel theft.''

Both women jerked around at the sound of Logan's voice. He was standing at the back door. They had been so intent on their own confrontation, they had not heard him enter.

Gail was the first to recover. ''I didn't mean to come up here and pry,'' she said stiffly, her attention remaining on her son. ''I've always tried not to interfere in your life. But I couldn't get that phone call out of my mind. I know how lonely this place can get.'' The implication in her last words brought a tinge of redness to her cheeks. Anger flashed in Logan's eyes, and his mother's teeth closed over her bottom lip as if she was afraid she might have said too much.

''You honestly thought I might be so desperate for female companionship I would hire a woman I couldn't trust to come here as my mistress?'' he growled.

Gail drew a shaky breath. ''I didn't know what to think. I know Marylin is spoiled and selfish and

I should take whatever she says warily, but I felt I should find out for certain.'' Her jaw tensed defensively. ''It's a mother's prerogative to worry about her son.''

As Logan continued to regard his mother coldly, Rachel read the fear in the woman's eyes. Gail McGreggor was afraid that he might not forgive her for this interference. There was no doubt in Rachel's mind that Gail McGreggor loved her son. And Rachel couldn't fault her for coming here to investigate. ''Your mother's right,'' she said calmly. Two pairs of brown eyes swung toward her. One held surprise, the other gratitude. ''In her place I would probably have done the same,'' she finished.

For a long moment a heavy silence filled the room as Logan's gaze traveled from one woman to the other. Then, giving a shrug as if to say he could not comprehend the female mind, he strode out of the kitchen.

As his steps echoed down the hall, Gail McGreggor said a little unevenly, ''Thank you.''

''I didn't come here to cause any trouble between Mr. James and his family,'' Rachel replied in her best proper-servant tone. Determined not to admit even to herself that Logan had had anything to do with her decision to accept this job, she added, ''I came here because I needed a job and I thought this ranch would be an interesting change of scenery.''

Gail McGreggor breathed a sigh of relief. "I appreciate your understanding." Uncertainty abruptly etched itself into her features. "I just hope Logan will be as generous. I'd better go find him."

Left alone in the kitchen, Rachel tried to concentrate on preparing dinner, but she couldn't help wondering what Gail McGreggor's reaction would have been if she and Logan *had* been having an intimate relationship. It was obvious she wouldn't be Mrs. McGreggor's first choice as a companion for Logan. *And you're not Logan's choice either,* she reminded herself curtly. This whole train of thought was immaterial. Angry that she continued to allow the man to occupy so much of her thoughts, she pushed him to the back of her mind and concentrated on cooking.

She served dinner to Logan and his mother in the dining room, waiting on the table in the formal manner she had learned at the Parry home.

During the meal, Mrs. McGreggor talked about what Logan's half brothers, half sister and stepfather were doing. Periodically, when Rachel entered to clear or serve, Mrs. McGreggor complimented her on her cooking.

Logan, however, said little. He seemed preoccupied, and Rachel began to wonder if he regretted offering her this job. He most definitely couldn't have guessed that Marylin would continue to try to cause trouble. The spoiled blonde might even be spreading rumors among his friends and acquaintances.

When Logan and his mother had finished their meal, Rachel sat down to eat alone in the kitchen. But the food stuck in her throat as the thought that she had become an embarrassment to Logan played through her mind.

Finally she rose from the table and began to wash the pots and pans. Maybe she should leave.

Hearing the kitchen door open, she turned to see Logan. He's probably come to tell me he's had second thoughts and wants me to go, she decided, seeing the grim expression on his face. She couldn't blame him. A person's reputation was important.

"I came to apologize for my mother's behavior this afternoon," he said as he came closer to her.

She wanted so much to reach out and touch the line of his jaw just once before she left and never saw him again. *It's probably a good thing he'd getting ready to fire you,* she told herself. Her reactions to him were much too disconcerting. "You should be glad you have a mother who cares," she replied. Unable to face him, she turned back to the pan she'd been washing.

Capturing her by the chin, he forced her to look up at him. "It does bother you, doesn't it?" he demanded.

His touch was spreading a warmth over her face and down her neck making it difficult for her to think. Afraid he might be able to see the effect he was having on her, she jerked free and returned her attention to the pan. "I told you I understood your mother's concern and I do."

"I'm not talking about my mother," he said gruffly. "I'm talking about your mother not caring about you."

Ugly memories flooded over her. "Of course it bothers me," she snapped. She turned to glare up at him. "I have feelings."

He traced the line of her jaw with the tip of his finger. "But you're very good at keeping them hidden," he replied softly.

Fresh currents of heat raced through Rachel. Again she jerked away from his touch. Why was she always admitting things to him she had tried not even to admit to herself? "I'm a private person," she said stiffly.

"So I've noticed," he replied dryly. For a long moment a silence hung between them while Rachel waited for him to suggest it would be best if she left. But instead, when he did speak again, he said, "Dinner was very good tonight."

"Thank you," she managed, telling herself that *she* should suggest that she leave. But before the words could form, he turned and left the room.

Standing at the sink, she stared out the kitchen window at the night. She considered going after Logan and telling him she was leaving. But her legs refused to move. The truth was that she wanted to stay. She felt safe here. Even more, from the moment she had arrived here, it seemed as if she'd found the home she'd been searching for all of her life.

"That is ridiculous!" she muttered. The feeling of safety was a result of Logan's coming to her aid at the Parry estate. "And he only did that because he thought it was the right thing to do," she reminded herself. As for this being the home she'd always been looking for, it wasn't. It was Logan's sanctuary, not hers. "But I am needed here at the moment," she reasoned. And she owed him her gratitude. So it was only right that she stay and take care of him for a while. "Just don't start thinking that it's anything permanent," she warned herself.

She was giving the counter a final wipe when Logan again entered the kitchen. "My mother has decided to return home tomorrow," he informed her. "She hates flying in the helicopter, so I'm going to drive her back to Billings. The rental car has to be returned, anyway. Hank will be flying in to get me. As long as we're there, we'll be picking up some supplies. You can fly in with Hank, or make me a list of what you want."

It occurred to Rachel that getting away from this ranch for a short while might be a good idea. She was growing much too attached to it. A trip into civilization might be just the thing she needed to get her emotions back on a more rational track. "I'll fly in with Hank," she said quickly.

A dry smile tilted one corner of Logan's mouth as if her response had been what he'd expected. "Getting bored out here already?"

"No," she replied honestly. Her gaze traveled around the kitchen. She wished she was. When the time came, leaving would be a great deal easier.

"I'm glad to hear that."

Startled by the relief she heard in his voice, she turned back toward him.

"You are a much better cook than I thought you would be," he added over his shoulder as he left the room.

A wave of disappointment washed over her. "Idiot!" she accused herself. For one brief moment she'd wanted to believe that his relief was deeper than merely the fear of losing a housekeeper. "And not only are you merely his housekeeper, you are merely his *temporary* housekeeper!"

She drew a shaky breath. Coming here the way she had on the spur of the moment had given this place a sort of fantasy image in her mind, she reasoned. Getting back to civilization, being around other people for a while, might bring her back to reality. She would probably even realize that she missed traffic, crowds and the noise of a city.

Chapter Six

Gail McGreggor had an early flight the next morning. She and Logan were up and gone before dawn. As Rachel cleaned up the breakfast dishes, the house seemed unpleasantly empty. "It's ridiculous I should be missing him," she muttered. As a general rule, Logan was out of the house nearly all day. There was nothing different about this morning except that he wasn't at the ranch. Still she couldn't shake the loneliness that taunted her. By the time Hank knocked on the door to tell her it was time to leave, she was ready and waiting.

Wanda flew into Billings with Rachel and Hank. She was going to visit her family while the others shopped for supplies.

During the flight, Rachel tried to concentrate on the scenery, but an anxiousness she couldn't shake persisted. When they landed and she saw Logan coming out to greet them, a rush of relief swept over her. Unable to deny it any longer, she had to admit that he was the reason she'd been so uneasy. She'd missed him! *This has got to stop,* she ordered herself.

Logan had kept the car his mother had rented. "Thought we'd take Wanda home first thing," he said to Hank, as the foursome walked toward the parking area.

Rachel was trailing a little behind and having a stern talk with herself. Logan had barely acknowledged her presence. *And that should tell you exactly where you stand with him.* But then she'd known all along that he had no interest in her. *These feelings you're having toward him are merely a natural attraction any woman might have for a good-looking man,* she insisted mentally. And, they would fade with time. *In fact, any day now, you should expect them to be gone,* she finished firmly.

When they reached Wanda's parents' home, Wanda's mother came out to greet them. "You're welcome to stay and visit with us," she said to Rachel. But behind Mrs. Stofer's polite smile, Rachel read hesitation in the woman's eyes.

"I thought Rachel should come with us," Logan interjected before Rachel could come up with a polite refusal. "This'll give her a chance for a firsthand look at what Billings has to offer."

"See you at lunchtime," Wanda said pointedly, letting the trio know that she expected them back for the meal.

"I'll drop Hank off," Logan replied. "I'm going to take Rachel out to lunch. I want her to get as much of the city life as possible so she doesn't start missing it when we get back to the ranch."

Wanda looked as if she was going to protest, but before she could say anything her mother slipped an arm around her shoulders. "Come on in. You look as if you need a nap."

Wanda glanced at Logan once again, then let herself be led into the house.

Rachel, too, glanced at Logan. It was obvious to her that he'd also seen the hesitation in Mrs. Stofer's eyes. *And so he's going to baby-sit me for the day so they won't be forced to endure the company of a stranger,* she realized.

During the remainder of the morning, she told herself it didn't bother her that Logan felt he had to play nursemaid—but it did. It would have been different if he'd really wanted to spend the time with her, but all morning she sensed an uneasiness about him and guessed that he would prefer being anywhere other than with her. By the time they left Hank at his mother-in-law's home, her nerves were on a brittle edge.

"I can find something to do to entertain myself for the afternoon," she said as they drove away. "Why don't you go back and have lunch with Hank and his in-laws?"

Logan looked at her impatiently. "I have no wish to spend the afternoon with Hank and his in-laws."

It suddenly occurred to Rachel that Logan might have a female friend he liked to visit when he was in Billings. The idea caused a hard knot to form in her stomach. Furious with herself for these continued reactions to the man, she said coolly, "I'm sure you must have a much more interesting way to spend the day than entertaining me. You can drop me off somewhere and I'll meet you at the airport."

Pulling over to the curb, Logan shifted the car into park and turned to face her. "Is that your way of telling me that you'd rather not spend the afternoon in my company?"

"I just figured maybe you had a friend you'd prefer spending your time with." The knot in her stomach tightened as she waited for him to confirm this.

But he didn't. Instead he said, "Your company's fine with me."

"You could have fooled me," she muttered dryly, then flushed at her outspokenness.

Logan raked his hand agitatedly through his hair. "The truth is I've been a little concerned about you this morning," he admitted gruffly.

Here it comes, Rachel thought, bracing herself to show only indifference. He's going to tell me that my being his housekeeper isn't going to work out and I'm fired. But considering the reactions she continued to have toward him, perhaps it was just as well.

Logan shifted his attention to the view beyond the front windshield. "I've been worried that you might be having second thoughts about returning to the ranch...that any minute now you're going to announce you've missed being in a town around other people and want to quit your job."

Rachel stared at his taut profile. He wasn't going to fire her. Instead, he was worried about her quitting. "I'm not having any second thoughts," she said firmly. *You should be having second, third and fourth thoughts,* her inner voice screamed at her. But she refused to listen.

Logan's jaw relaxed. "Glad to hear that," he said, shifting the car into gear and pulling onto the road. "I hate the idea of eating my own cooking."

He hadn't even looked at her. Self-directed anger again filled her as another wave of disappointment washed over her. She'd been holding her breath, waiting for him to admit that he liked having her around. But it wasn't her, it was her cooking that concerned him. *And you knew that!* she scolded herself. *Think boss and employee and nothing more.*

By the time they entered a busy café a little while later, she was certain she had herself under complete control.

"Logan James, you're a sight for sore eyes," a pretty brunette waitress greeted him.

Bile rose in Rachel's throat. So much for control, she chided herself. *You're jealous,* her inner voice mocked her. *I am not,* she denied vehemently.

"How are the kids?" Logan asked as the waitress led them to a table and handed them menus.

"Charlie's walking and Marty started kindergarten this year," she replied. "My husband keeps talking about having a third. I told him that when the doctors devised a way he could carry the baby and give birth, then we'd have another one." Laughing lightly, she added, "Be back for your order in a few minutes." Then she hurried away to another table.

Rachel hated admitting how relieved she was to learn that the woman was married. *Your emotions are in one heck of a muddle,* she grumbled silently as she glanced at the menu.

"I know you didn't get a good view of the country between here and my ranch the night we arrived from New York," Logan said conversationally. "What did you think of it when you finally got to see it this morning?"

She turned toward him to find she had his full attention. "It was beautiful," she replied honestly.

"Guess you were a little surprised by how isolated we are out there on the ranch," he continued evenly.

She shrugged. "It's peaceful out there."

He smiled crookedly with pleasure. "I think so, too." Then he turned his attention back to the menu.

Rachel wished he wouldn't smile like that. It caused a warm curling sensation that spread all the way to her toes. Scowling at herself, she, too, turned her attention to the menu.

After placing her order, she sat staring out the window. The problem was she was getting too used to Logan's company. It almost felt natural being with him, as if she wasn't totally complete without him. Her thoughts turned to the daily routine they'd established since her arrival at the ranch.

After her first day there, they'd started having their meals together. He'd insisted that it was the most practical arrangement. Each morning during breakfast, he would tell her his schedule for the day so she could plan the rest of the meals around it. He'd also give instructions for any calls he needed her to make or any errands he wanted her to take care of. As soon as Wanda had been relieved of her duties at the main house, Hank had begun having lunch at his own place with his wife, leaving Rachel and Logan alone for all three meals. The problem was they had very little to discuss during the noon and evening meals.

Following their nearly silent lunch on the third day of this arrangement, her food had sat on her stomach like a rock for the entire afternoon. Her usual solution of simply shutting out the rest of the world hadn't worked. Logan's presence was not easy for her to ignore. In fact, she found it impossible. By dinnertime, she was ready to admit that she couldn't handle eating in almost total silence with him for two meals a day. Action had to be taken.

"How is Miss Rita doing?" she'd asked, searching for a topic she thought might interest him.

"She's doing fine," he'd replied, looking surprised by the question.

"When is her baby due?" she'd persisted.

"It's called a foal," he corrected.

"What's called a foal?" she asked, deciding to play dumb. At least that would get another sentence out of him.

"The newborn horse," he'd replied. "It's a filly if it's a female, and a colt if it's a male."

So far so good, she'd told herself. Not only was he answering her, he was elaborating. "When you were talking to Hank, I got the impression that you're concerned about this particular birth," she'd coaxed.

A shadow of anxiousness clouded his eyes. "I am a little," he confessed. "Her last foal was a breech birth and caused her a lot of trouble."

Rachel could see him relaxing. His shoulders became less tense and his drawl became more pronounced. "I believe I once heard Justin mention that you raise these horses to sell?" she prompted.

He nodded and, with no more coaxing, spent the rest of the meal telling her about the operation of the ranch.

After that, their mealtimes had been less of a strain. She found she could easily prod him into telling her about his activities of the day. Even when he'd had a bad day, his jaw would relax and a gleam would come into his eyes when he talked about his ranch. There was love there. Even more, there was commitment.

Rachel glanced at the cowboy seated across from her at the café table. He was a rarity in her life—someone a person could depend on. Her jaw tensed. *I do not need anyone to depend on but myself,* she told herself curtly.

"You look like a woman with something on her mind," Logan said, breaking into her thoughts.

"It was nothing important," she replied.

For a moment he studied her as if he was going to challenge this statement, then he gave a small shrug and said in an easy drawl, "I thought we'd do a little shopping for you this afternoon."

She frowned in surprise. "Me?"

"I've noticed that you only have a couple of pairs of jeans. You need at least one more pair and a couple more work shirts. And you need boots and

a hat." His jaw firmed with resolve. "I'm buying."

She was having a hard-enough time keeping her
thoughts about him in the proper perspective. Letting him buy her clothes seemed much too personal. "I have money. I can buy my own clothes."

"You didn't pay for the uniform you wore when
working for Justin, did you?" he questioned, his
manner becoming brusquely businesslike.

"No, but..." She started to point out that she'd
left the uniform behind. Jeans, boots, shirts and a
hat were things she'd take with her when she left
Montana.

"Then consider these things part of the uniform
for your current job," he replied.

Their food arrived at that moment and he began
to eat. His expression indicated he considered the
subject closed.

Mentally Rachel promised herself that she'd keep
a total and pay him back.

As soon as they'd finished eating, Logan drove
them to a clothing store.

"Well, if it ain't Logan James." An elderly man,
partially bald, dressed in jeans, a western-cut shirt,
a string tie and cowboy boots, came striding down
the aisle to greet them as they entered. "Ain't seen
you in my store in quite a spell." He shook hands
with Logan in the manner of an old friend, then
smiled at Rachel. "And where'd you find this
pretty-looking gal? I'm sure I haven't seen her

around before. I'd remember a pair of green eyes like that.''

"She's my new housekeeper," Logan replied. "Rachel Hadley, meet Buck Langely."

"Pleased to meet you," Rachel said.

"Pleased to meet you, too," Buck replied, adding with a grin, "You sure must brighten up that ranch a bit." Then he turned his attention back to Logan and his grin broadened. "I heard Wanda was in the family way. But I never expected you to find anyone so pretty to take her place."

"Miss Hadley has been a surprise to me, too," Logan replied.

"Right pleasant one is my guess," the elderly man returned with a knowing wink.

Logan scowled. "She's a very good cook," he said sharply.

For a moment the storekeeper looked uneasy, then recovering quickly from the rebuff, he grinned and said, "Good thing for you. A man's stomach is important. Now, what can I do for you today?"

"Miss Hadley is in need of a few things," Logan replied.

A couple of hours later, Rachel had new shirts, new jeans, a new pair of boots, some heavy socks to wear with them and a Stetson hat. "I feel like a real cowgirl," she said, looking down at her boots.

"Not quite," Logan said. He set her hat on her head. "Now you look like a real cowgirl."

He grinned that crooked grin of his and Rachel's heart lurched. Quickly she diverted her attention back to her boots, "These are going to take a little getting used to," she said.

Buck had been ringing up the bill. He glanced toward Logan speculatively. "Used to be when a man bought a woman boots and a hat it was the same as putting his brand on her."

"I'm not too sure any man will ever be able to put his brand on Miss Hadley," Logan replied coolly as he paid the man.

Rachel's back stiffened. Clearly Logan didn't consider her marriage material. Well, she'd known his opinion all along, she reminded herself, angry for even caring what Logan thought. She glanced at the storekeeper. She wanted to make certain he put the receipt in the bag so she would know how much she owed Logan.

When they reached the airport, they found Hank and Wanda already there waiting for them. Wanda's mother and youngest sister were there, also, and Rachel noticed that Wanda's mother looked uneasy. She braced herself to face the woman's suspicious glances. But instead Mrs. Stofer smiled at her.

"I wish Wanda could stay with me until the baby is due," she said anxiously, "but a wife should be with her husband." A pleading quality entered her voice. "You will keep a close eye on her, won't you, Rachel? You don't know how nervous I've been thinking about her being alone during the day. I've been so worried that she'll go into labor and the men will be out working and she won't be able to reach them.''

"Hank and Logan work it so that one of them is always where they can hear the bell,'' Wanda assured her mother in a tone that implied they'd had this discussion a hundred times before.

It pleased Rachel that the woman was willing to ask for her aid. Her cynical side guessed that Mrs. Stofer would have asked the devil himself if she thought he would help her daughter, but that didn't matter. "I'll keep an eye on her,'' she promised. As she headed for the helicopter, again she was bothered by how much she wanted to be accepted by these people. She'd spent a lifetime trying not to care if the people around her wanted her company. *But it's not as if you're going to be staying,* she reminded herself.

Later, as Logan landed the helicopter back at the ranch, a warm, welcoming feeling spread over her as if she'd come home. *This is not your home. It's merely a place of temporary employment,* she admonished herself. But the sensation prevailed.

"I'm just tired,'' she muttered when she was alone in her room. It wasn't reasonable to feel so attached to a place she'd been for so short a time.

A sharp knock sounded on her bedroom door. It was Logan. "I'm going out to check on the stock,'' he informed her. "It's been a long day. You take the rest of it off. I'll just grab a sandwich for dinner when I come back.''

Standing in the doorway of her room, she watched him as he strode down the hall. She was tired. Sitting down in front of the television with a sandwich and propping her legs up sounded good. But it was already dark outside and the wind had taken on its nightly chill. Logan would need a hot meal when he came back in.

As she started the potatoes baking and made a salad, she told herself she was doing this because it was her job. She didn't want to admit, even to herself, how much she wanted to see that Logan was properly cared for.

He looked surprised when he came in and found her cooking. He smiled gratefully. "I'm glad you decided to fix something hot. Truth is, it was cold out there and I'm a mite hungrier than I thought I would be.''

Rachel experienced a rush of pleasure. *It's dangerous to care so much,* she warned herself. But the feeling remained.

"I suppose I sound like a dull clod, but I'm always glad to get back to this ranch,'' he said as they sat eating. "Even after being away only part of a day.''

"This place can get into a person's blood,'' Rachel replied, then clamped her mouth shut when she realized what she'd said.

His gaze narrowed. "You think so?''

Afraid he might read in her face how fond she had become of his ranch, she lowered her head and pretended to be more interested in cutting a piece of meat than in their conversation. "It's obvious that you, Hank and Wanda love it here. As for me, I prefer not to become too attached to any one place."

"Or to any one person," he added.

"Or to any one person," she confirmed, more for herself than for him.

"Sounds like a lonely way to live," Logan said in an easy drawl that neither condemned nor encouraged.

It was, she admitted to herself. But until now it had never felt this lonely. "It's a safe way to live," she stated.

"Maybe," he conceded.

Her food had lost its appeal. The pieces of meat tasted like cardboard and felt like rocks as they hit her stomach. But she forced herself to finish. She didn't want him guessing how much this conversation bothered her. He was merely making small talk to pass the time. She was sure that he'd be stunned to discover how she really felt. She was having a hard time believing it herself.

Chapter Seven

It took some work and a great deal of self-admonition, but by the next morning, Rachel was sure she had her reactions to Logan and his ranch under control. She had reinforced her wall of reserve. Once again, she thought of her job as merely a temporary stopover to somewhere else. As for Logan, she promised herself she would no longer allow herself any personal feelings for him.

Neutral was what she wanted to feel toward him. It was what she was *determined* to feel toward him. During breakfast, she worked hard to maintain an indifferent attitude. It wasn't easy. When he first entered the kitchen, she felt a warm stirring inside. *What you're experiencing is nothing but trouble,* she warned herself.

For his part, Logan's manner toward her remained the same as always—that of a boss maintaining a hospitable but impersonal relationship with an employee.

"And that's the way I want it," she said firmly, standing at the sink watching him through the window as he walked toward the barns.

Returning her attention to the dishes, she ordered herself to put him out of her mind and concentrate on something else. But by midmorning she had the house sparkling and was again standing at the kitchen window looking out toward the corrals wondering where Logan was and what he was doing.

"Bake some cookies!" she ordered herself, determined not to think about him. Since she'd outgrown adolescent crushes at around the age of fourteen, she'd never allowed any male to occupy her mind so fully.

As she started to move away, she saw him come out of the barn leading a saddled horse. The animal seemed to be fighting the reins—not a lot, but a little. Logan led it into a corral and began walking it around the enclosure.

"Go bake your cookies," she ordered herself again when she found her legs had refused to move. She enjoyed watching Logan work. She enjoyed watching Logan. "You're behaving like you're one brick short of a load," she warned herself. Still, she remained at the window.

She saw Hank come out and perch himself on the top rail of the corral fence. He was shaking his head as if he disapproved of what Logan was doing. Then she saw Logan move to the horse's side. He patted the animal and seemed to be talking to it. Suddenly, in one swift movement, he mounted it.

For a moment the horse froze as if stunned by this added weight, then it began to buck.

Rachel's breath locked in her lungs. Logan's arms looked as if they were being jerked from their sockets as his whole body was jarred and bounced. She winced at the thought of the pain he had to be feeling. Then the animal gave a wild lunge and Logan's hold broke. He flew off the horse and landed on the ground so hard the impact sent up a cloud of dust. In a flash, Hank was in the corral waving his hat at the animal to keep it away from Logan.

Rachel was halfway to the corral before she even realized she'd left the kitchen.

The horse had calmed down as soon as it had divested itself of its unwanted rider. By the time Rachel reached the corral, the animal was standing several feet away, warily watching Hank and Logan.

"Are you all right, boss?" Hank asked worriedly, holding a hand out to Logan.

Logan didn't accept the offered aid. Instead he remained sprawled on the ground. "I just need a minute. Got the wind knocked out of me real good," he said between gasps for air.

Hank shook his head. "I thought you had more sense than that. You knew that horse wasn't ready to be rode yet."

"Guess my patience is a little thin today," Logan muttered, easing himself into a sitting position.

"I'd say it was your common sense that was thin today," Rachel interjected, coming closer. She'd told herself to be quiet, watch for a moment, assure herself that Logan was all right and then go back to the house. But instead she heard herself saying, "What did you think you were doing? Trying to get yourself killed?" She'd meant for this to sound like a reprimand, instead it came out shakily.

Logan looked up at her in surprise. "It was just a minor disagreement," he said in an easy drawl. He reached toward Hank, and this time when Hank held out a hand, Logan caught it and let Hank help him to his feet.

Rachel tried to will herself to say no more, but her fear was still too strong. Logan was taking all this much too nonchalantly. "You could have broken your neck!" Her gaze raked over him trying to see if there were any visible injuries.

"My thoughts exactly," Hank seconded, still regarding Logan with a puzzled expression.

Logan glanced at Hank. "Why don't you put Dancer back in his stall," he suggested.

"Think I'd better," Hank replied. "It's going to take an extra week or two now to get him ready." As he moved toward the horse, he again shook his head as if he still couldn't understand what had gotten into Logan.

"I think you should come up to the house and let me call a doctor," Rachel suggested worriedly, her gaze never leaving Logan.

Studying her narrowly, he smiled that crooked smile of his. "A man could get the impression that you care."

Rachel swallowed. *You're doing a rotten job of keeping your feelings under control,* she berated herself. Even worse, he's going to guess how attracted you are to him. She took a deep breath, then faced him squarely. "If you get yourself killed I'm out of a job."

The crooked smile vanished. He studied her for a moment longer, then shifted his attention to his jeans and took a couple of swipes at them to knock off the dust. When he straightened, his manner was once again cool and distant. "Speaking of jobs, guess I'd better get back to work."

"Me, too," she responded, ordering herself to start moving toward the house. But as he turned to walk away, she noticed he was limping. "Maybe you should come up to the house and rest for a while," she coaxed.

He turned back toward her, his expression shuttered. "That'd only cause the muscles to stiffen. It's best to keep moving."

She fought to keep her tone impersonal. "If you say so." She forced a shrug, then turned away. Suddenly a horrifying thought struck her and she swung around. "I hope you're not going to try riding another bucking bronco just to keep your muscles limber."

The crooked smile returned. "Nope. My body may be a little bruised, but my brain wasn't so badly jogged that I don't have any sense left."

He's going to guess how you feel if you don't walk away now, she warned herself. "Good," she said sharply, then strode back to the house.

Alone in the kitchen, she discovered her hands were shaking. "I would have been as concerned if he had been a total stranger," she informed the emptiness around her, afraid to admit even to herself how terrified she had been for him. Still, she found herself wandering over to the window and glancing toward the corrals to assure herself that Logan hadn't decided to try his luck again on the horse.

"Bake your cookies and put that man out of your mind," she ordered herself.

But barring Logan James from her mind this time proved to be impossible. She kept glancing at the clock and realized she was waiting for him to come in for lunch so she could assure herself that he hadn't injured himself more seriously than he'd admitted.

When he did come in, she couldn't resist watching him cross the room to see if he was still limping. To her relief, he wasn't. Once assured, she returned her attention to putting their lunch on the table.

"I've been wondering if you know how to ride a horse," he said conversationally as they sat down to eat.

Her dry sense of humor surfaced. "If you're planning on asking me to try to tame that bronco for you, forget it."

He laughed and she felt her heart lurch. It was such a warm, friendly sound. "Nope," he assured her. He smiled that quirky smile of his again. "I've been thinking that maybe you might like to see a little more of my ranch from ground level."

"I would," she admitted, hoping that being out on the vast range might cause her to feel uncomfortable about the isolation. She needed something to make leaving easier. "But I don't know how to ride."

"Then I guess I'll have to teach you," he said. "A person needs to know how to ride if they're living on a ranch."

It wasn't an offer, it was a statement of intent. But she didn't balk. She'd always wanted to learn to ride. "Fine," she replied. "As long as you pick a horse that's gentler than the one you were on this morning.''

He regarded her speculatively. ''Personally I think you might be a match for him, but I've got another horse in mind for you. She's gentle as a lamb. You'll probably intimidate the hell out of her.''

Rachel frowned down at her food. It was obvious he thought of her as being tough as leather. Well, life had taught her to be that way—at least on the outside. Still, it bothered her that he had such an unflattering opinion of her. Frustrated with the muddle he made of her emotions, she again wished she had a thicker skin where he was concerned.

When they finished eating, he insisted on helping her with the dishes. ''The sooner you get done in here, the sooner we can get on with your lesson,'' he said as he carried plates to the sink.

She was certain she detected a note of impatience in his voice. He was probably already regretting his offer. Well, she'd never forced her company on anyone before and she wasn't going to start now. If he wanted a way out, she'd give it to him. ''If you've thought of something else you need to do this afternoon, my riding lesson can wait.''

''Nope,'' he replied firmly. ''I haven't got anything else that needs to be done.''

It had taken only a few minutes to clean up after lunch. Then, after telling her that he was going to go to the barn and saddle their horses, he sent her to her room to fetch a heavy jacket and a pair of her driving gloves.

When she reached the barn she found Hank saddling a gray mare. Logan was cinching the saddle on his black stallion.

After making certain the saddle was secure, Hank handed her the reins.

"Lead her outside," Logan instructed, keeping his horse in its stall until she passed.

"I'm a little nervous about this, girl," Rachel said to the horse, reaching up and stroking its neck as they walked. "So please behave."

"You won't have any trouble with that one," Logan informed her, as they left the barn. "Wait there," he ordered as soon as they were outside. Leading his horse over to the corral, he threw the reins around the top rail, then returned to Rachel.

He instructed her on the proper way to mount and gave her a helping hand into the stirrup. Once she was seated in the saddle, he adjusted both stirrups, telling her how to use her legs and knees to keep her balance and to keep herself from being jostled too much.

Rachel concentrated on everything he was saying, but it wasn't easy. She was acutely aware of his touch each time his hands came into contact with her body. It had been difficult enough when he brushed against her leg while adjusting the length of the stirrups. But when he held on to her calf to show her how to move her leg, a trail of fire raced through her. "I think I've got the idea," she assured him quickly.

Nodding, he walked over to the black stallion and mounted. Guiding his horse back to stand beside hers, he explained how to use the reins, then asked, "Are you ready to give it a try?"

Again she'd noticed an uneasiness about him as if he wasn't certain he really felt comfortable doing this. It wasn't clearly evident, but it was there. She was tempted to tell him that she'd changed her mind and didn't want his lesson. But she did want it. She wanted to ride out onto the open rugged range more than she'd ever wanted to do anything. And, she'd better get her fill of it this trip, she told herself, because he'd probably never offer to take her again. "I'm ready."

Logan gave his horse a nudge with his heels and it began to walk. Rachel gave her horse a similar nudge and, to her relief, it began to move also, pacing itself so that it remained parallel to Logan's stallion but not crowding it.

As they left the outbuildings and corrals behind, Rachel marveled at the openness of land. She took a deep breath of the clear, crisp air. Never had she experienced such a feeling of freedom.

They had been riding in silence for about twenty minutes when Logan turned toward her. "Well, what do you think of my ranch now?" he asked.

He spoke in an easy drawl as if this was merely a conversational question and her answer held little significance. But she noticed that his eyes were guarded. "It's beautiful," she replied. Her gaze left him to scan the landscape. "It makes a person feel good just to see it."

The uneasiness she'd sensed in him disappeared and the guardedness left his eyes. He smiled. "That's the way I feel. I'm glad you agree."

Rachel studied his rough-featured face. It had been important to him that she like his ranch. *The same way it's important to a child that the people he shows his favorite toy to like it,* she reasoned, refusing to allow herself to believe that his pleasure was due to anything more than pride in his ranch.

As if to confirm this, he added, "I wouldn't want you bolting and leaving me to find a new housekeeper at this late a date."

In spite of what she'd just told herself, a wave of disappointment swept over her. She'd hoped she meant more to him than merely a housekeeper until Wanda could return to the job. *Silly woman!* she admonished herself. Determined to lighten her mood with a bit of humor, she cautioned dryly, "Don't say the word 'bolt' while I'm sitting on a horse. You might give it ideas."

He grinned. "I like a woman with a sense of humor."

Rachel had to close her teeth over her bottom lip to keep from smiling too broadly. Her gaze met his and she felt herself being drawn into the dark depths of his eyes. She began to feel light-headed and realized that she was holding her breath. *You're acting like a schoolgirl,* she chided herself, taking a deep breath and shifting her gaze back to the barren landscape. *A person would think you'd never received a compliment before. I've got to get my reactions to this man under control!*

"We should be getting back," Logan said, breaking the silence that had again fallen between them.

She heard impatience in his voice. The pleasure the compliment had brought vanished. He was already tired of her company. "Sounds like a good idea to me," she replied coolly.

He said nothing during the ride back and she made no attempt at conversation.

"If you feel sore, you should go soak in a hot tub for a while," he suggested as they dismounted at the stables. "I tried not to keep you out too long."

"I feel fine," she assured him, handing him her reins. *As if he really cared,* she added to herself.

"Good."

He looked honestly relieved and she hated herself for being so catty. It wasn't his fault he wasn't attracted to her.

"I thought we'd go out for a little longer tomorrow," he added.

Pride caused her shoulders to stiffen. "I know you have other things you'd rather do." She'd meant to stop there, but "I don't want to bore you again with my company" slipped out.

He regarded her with an expression of mild surprise. "Your company doesn't bore me. Is tomorrow after lunch okay with you?"

"Sure, fine," she managed, feeling a flush developing on her neck and moving up. Turning abruptly away from him, she strode toward the house. She felt like an idiot. She'd practically admitted that she cared whether or not he liked having her around.

For the rest of the afternoon, she fretted about what she'd said. Revealing herself like that made her feel vulnerable, and that made her uneasy. But when Logan came in for dinner he made no mention about her concern regarding his attitude toward her company.

Instead he spent the meal telling her about some plans he had for the ranch. For the first time since her arrival, she felt as if he was truly inviting her into his world.

The strength of her desire to be a part of that world frightened her. *You're going to be very disappointed if you ever let yourself believe that could happen,* she cautioned herself. Afraid to face him for fear that her inner turmoil might show, she feigned intense interest in her dessert as she said, "I'm sure what you have in mind will be a tremendous success."

"I hope I haven't bored you," he said stiffly.

Her back muscles tightened. Was he ridiculing her? She lifted her head to look at him, but there was no amusement in his eyes. Instead he was watching her guardedly. "No, you didn't bore me," she assured him.

He smiled then and said, "It's nice to have someone to talk to."

Rachel's heart began to pound double time. "I enjoyed listening to you." Immediately she lowered her gaze back to her dessert. That didn't sound too bright, she berated herself.

"My father used to say that a woman who's a good listener is worth her weight in gold," Logan said. "He must have been right. Truth is, talking this out has steered me in a clearer direction."

Her heart beat even more wildly. "I'm glad," she replied, continuing to feign interest in her dessert. She still felt foolish and was afraid to face him. He might see how much his compliments meant to her.

"That was a fine dinner," he said as he pushed his chair back from the table and rose to his feet. Starting across the room, he added over his shoulder, "I'll be in my study."

Rachel sat dumbly as he left. She couldn't believe how much his simple compliment had meant to her. Her heart was still racing and a flush of pleasure had reddened her cheeks.

"Justin used to compliment you on being a good listener, too," she reminded herself, determined to keep this exchange with Logan within the proper perspective. He would probably have given Hank the same compliment if it'd been Hank sitting in her chair. All he needed was someone to listen. "You're no one special to him," she softly informed herself. "And don't go thinking you could be. You'll only get hurt."

Chapter Eight

During the next few weeks, Rachel's riding lessons became a fairly regular event. After the fourth day, Logan had declared her a natural horsewoman. She'd had no trouble following his instructions and was already maintaining her seat in the saddle like an experienced hand.

There had been a couple of days when Logan hadn't been able to take her out because of work that needed to be done. On those days she'd been tempted to go out by herself. Instead of feeling like a foreigner in this wild, untamed land, she felt akin to it, as if it was the natural habitat she had been seeking all of her life.

"Maybe when my job here is over, I'll find another one on a ranch like this," she mused as she worked around the kitchen on a particularly bright, crisp April morning. "But not in Montana." She didn't want to be where she might run into Logan again. As hard as she tried, she couldn't entirely rid herself of the attraction she felt toward him. And his new attitude toward her wasn't helping. After her first riding lesson he'd begun talking to her more, his manner casual and friendly, the way it was with Hank and Wanda.

At first she'd continued to maintain her reserve. But one night at dinner, he'd brought the walls crashing down.

He'd been talking about purchasing some wild mustangs when he stopped abruptly in midsentence. Impatience flickered in his eyes. "You remind me of a mannequin."

Rachel had been trying very hard not to wonder what it would feel like to run her hand over his unshaven jaw. Early that morning, one of the stallions had been spooked and the horse's leg had been injured. Through an intercom hooked up to the house, she and Logan had been awakened by the ruckus. He'd rushed out to calm the horse and afterward just continued with his day without shaving. Now there was dark stubble on his face, and she was mentally ordering herself not to think about how it might feel beneath her palm. "What?" she'd said, the sharpness in his voice putting her on the defensive.

He'd regarded her grimly. "I feel as if I'm talking to a mannequin. You're sitting there with that vacant expression on your face again. Were you simply being polite when you told me you were interested in hearing about my day?"

He was right about her expression. Her jaws hurt from trying to keep her features neutral. "I am interested," she'd assured him. She'd tried to relax her facial muscles, but he was studying her so closely his scrutiny was making her even more tense.

Ignoring her disclaimer, he'd continued to regard her with an impatient scowl. "It's like there's an invisible shield you keep around yourself. Do you distrust people so much you won't even allow someone to be your friend?"

With her nerves already taut, his disapproving tone caused her control to snap. "I have good reason not to trust people," she'd said as memories she normally kept locked in the back of her mind suddenly assailed her.

"I realize that your mother and stepfather treated you badly—"

"Do you think I let the actions of those two totally guide my life?" she'd demanded. A bitterness entered her voice. "When I got out of reform school I was sent to a foster home. That suited me just fine. As far as I was concerned, if I never saw my mother or stepfather again, I could die happy. But I thought I still had friends among the kids I'd gone to school with. I learned real fast how wrong I was. The girls wouldn't have anything to do with me..." The bitterness increased. "The boys did come to see me, but only because they assumed that my doing time had made me loose." Even as the words poured out, she couldn't believe she was making these admissions to him. She'd never allowed anyone even to guess how hurt she'd been.

Humiliation swept over her. She rose from her chair and stood with her shoulders squared. "I suppose I've become cynical. But it's been my experience that most people tend to be fair-weather friends," she'd finished stiffly.

Not wanting to face him any longer, she'd left the kitchen and headed for her room. She needed some time alone. Behind her she heard his bootsteps. The temptation was strong to break into a run, but pride refused to allow that.

"Rachel, wait," he'd ordered gruffly. As he spoke, he caught up with her and his hand closed over her shoulder.

For a second she'd considered jerking free and making a dash for her room. But that would have been cowardly. Besides, she hadn't said anything to be ashamed of. She just wasn't used to revealing herself so completely. She'd turned toward him, her mask of cool reserve again on her face.

"Has it ever occurred to you that you might be associating with the wrong kind of people?" he asked.

"I suppose," she conceded. Challenge suddenly flickered in her eyes. "But how am I supposed to tell the 'right' people from the 'wrong' people? I trusted Justin and look what happened." Her hands balled into fists. She'd done it again! Why was she always telling this man things she didn't like admitting even to herself?

"I guess there's no certain way to tell who you can trust or who you can't," he replied. His jaw hardened as he met her gaze. "I guess that's just a chance you have to take. But I can promise you that if you want my friendship, it's yours, and I'm not the kind of person who'll turn away from you in times of trouble."

Every instinct had told her this was the truth. But she was still frightened of letting him get any closer. "I'm sure you're steadfast, loyal and true. But it might be best if we kept our relationship strictly employee-employer," she said levelly.

He searched her face. "Are you so afraid of being hurt by others that you refuse to allow yourself to have even friendships? Or has your past turned your feelings to stone?"

She wanted so much to be his friend. *You want to be more than just his friend,* her inner voice corrected, and she couldn't deny this. But friendship was all he was offering and it was all he would ever offer. "Sometimes I wish my feelings had been turned to stone," she heard herself saying. Stunned, she jerked free from his touch and took a step back. "That would have saved me a lot of disappointments," she added, not wanting him to get the slightest hint that he might be the main reason for this wish. Again the need to escape from him was too strong to deny. Turning away, she started toward her room.

But before she'd gone two steps, he caught her by the arm. "I'll abide by your wishes," he said, forcing her to turn and look at him. "But if you ever change your mind and want my friendship, I'll be here." Without waiting for a response, he released her, then returned to the kitchen.

Alone in her room, she'd paced the floor. The thought of letting down her guard was scary, but she was tempted. For the time that she was here, it *would* be nice to have Logan as a friend, to be able to laugh and joke with him the way Hank and Wanda did. Besides, to continue to refuse his friendship would make her look as though she was either too afraid to cope with the simplest of relationships, or she was so cold she honestly didn't care about others.

"I can do this," she'd told her image in the mirror. "It might even be easier to be on friendly terms with him than to continue this charade of indifference. All I have to do is remember that we're going to be friends and nothing more."

She'd forced her features into an expression of confidence. "I can do it!"

But it hadn't been easy. In fact, it had been much harder than she'd ever imagined. The more she got to know Logan the more she liked him. Beneath his rugged exterior he was a gentle man, a good man. He wasn't perfect. There were days when his temper would flare. At those times, she found herself making excuses for him. A friend always makes allowances for a friend, she'd tell herself.

But as she stood at the counter on this particularly sunny day late in April, she was worried. Just the thought of leaving caused a hard knot in her stomach. "You've got to think of this job as temporary," she ordered herself. "And when you leave, you've got to put it all behind you."

The ringing of the phone interrupted her.

"Rachel, I think I'm in labor," Wanda said even before Rachel had a chance to say hello.

"I'll be right over as soon as I ring the bell for Hank and Logan," Rachel responded, plopping the bread she had been kneading into a bowl, then rinsing off her hands as she spoke.

"Thanks," Wanda said with a relieved sigh, then gasped as if having a sudden pain.

Rachel dropped the receiver into its cradle and raced for the door. She'd planned on reacting calmly when this time came, but her heart was pounding rapidly. She was excited and she was scared. They were nearly an hour's helicopter ride from the hospital. "First babies take a long time," she muttered to herself. She'd always heard this and she hoped it was true.

Pausing on the porch, she rang the bell several times. Satisfied that if Logan or Hank was within hearing distance the ring would be heard, she jogged over to Wanda's.

The redhead met her at the door. "I'm sure we have plenty of time," Wanda said. "The pains are still about fifteen minutes apart."

"You should have called me earlier," Rachel admonished, wondering how soon the baby would be born. She'd once gone to see a film on how to deliver a baby, but she had no confidence about actually being able to do it.

Wanda laughed. "You look more panicked than Hank."

Rachel had heard rapid bootsteps hit the porch. Hank rushed past her to his wife's side.

"Is it time?" he demanded, his voice filled with anxious protectiveness.

"Looks like it to me," Logan said, as Wanda suddenly began panting in an effort to control the pain of a contraction. In his easy drawl he added with a grin, "Don't you worry, Wanda. If the baby decides to come faster than normal, we can land the 'copter in a field and Hank and I can deliver it. We've helped dozens of new foals into the world."

In spite of her pain, Wanda returned his grin. "Now that's a comforting thought."

But Rachel didn't have any comforting thoughts for the next hour. It wasn't until Wanda was safely in the hospital in Billings that she finally breathed a sigh of relief. Even then the relief was short-lived. Now came the waiting for the birth.

Hank was allowed to be with Wanda, but Logan and Rachel were relegated to the waiting area. Rachel had offered to call Wanda's family, but Wanda had asked her to hold off phoning. "My mother would be a nervous wreck waiting," the redhead had explained. "It'd be better to call her after the baby is born. She can't be with me in the delivery room, anyway, and that'll save her the pacing."

"Wanda's going to be just fine," Logan said reassuringly. He was sitting in one of the chairs, his long legs stretched out in front of him and crossed at the ankle.

Rachel glanced at him. He looked so relaxed. She, on the other hand, was as tense as a bowstring. Unable to sit, she had been wandering around the waiting room, pausing occasionally to look out the window, picking up a magazine, then immediately putting it down. She told herself several times to sit, but she was too tense. "I'm doing the pacing for Mrs. Stofer," she joked.

"For someone who has spent a lot of years making it a practice not to let anyone get too close, you've adapted real well to caring about people," he observed.

His words stung. He obviously thought she'd gone through a major portion of her life with a cold, uncaring attitude. She faced him with proud dignity. "I've never stopped caring about people. I simply feel most have only their own interests at heart." For the past weeks she'd been reminding herself of this premise daily in her attempt to keep Logan's friendly manner toward her in the proper perspective. He needed a housekeeper and it was more pleasant to have one he was on relaxed terms with, she'd told herself a zillion times. That was all that was behind his offer of friendship.

He frowned skeptically. "I don't understand how you can claim to care about people when you think their motives are basically selfish."

"I accept the selfishness as part of human nature and try not to hold it against them. It saves me from being disappointed in people." Her jaw tensed. She was baring her soul to him again. She walked to the window and feigned intense interest in the scene beyond.

"I suppose you might have a point there," he muttered.

For several minutes an uneasy silence hung between them. Rachel guessed he must think she was one of the most cynical people in the world. But that cynicism had gotten her through a lot of difficult times. Trying not to care about what he thought of her, she concentrated on wondering how Wanda was doing. In the silence the minutes seemed like hours. She glanced at her watch. It was barely a minute since she'd last checked. "I wish Hank would come out here and tell us what's happening," she said, finally unable to endure the silence any longer.

"I've always found it's best not to worry until you know you've got something to worry about," Logan replied. "It saves a person from a lot of anxious moments."

"I'm not really worried," Rachel admitted, returning her attention to the view beyond the window. "It's more like a nervous excitement." She smiled self-consciously. "There's something very special about a new life entering the world."

"I've always thought so," Logan replied.

Rachel felt a prickling on her neck and knew he was studying her. What had she said this time to garner his scrutiny?

"And if you honestly believe what you just said, you can't be as much of a cynic as you would have me believe," he added, answering her unspoken question.

Life would be a lot easier if she was as cynical as she tried to be, she mused. Aloud she said, "I've never claimed to be perfect."

He laughed gently. "I like a woman who can joke about herself."

His soft laughter caused a warmth to envelop Rachel. The image of him holding her in his arms as he looked deep into her eyes and said what he'd just said suddenly filled her mind. . . .

The delivery of Wanda's baby took several hours. But finally Hank came into the waiting room with the grin of a proud new father on his face. "It's a boy," he announced. "Both he and Wanda are doing great."

"Are we going to get to see this new addition?" Logan asked.

Rachel had been going to ask the same question. She glanced toward Logan and saw reflected in his eyes the same excitement and interest she was feeling.

"Sure thing," Hank replied, and led them to the nursery.

"He's adorable," Rachel said, and meant it.

Hank stayed for a few minutes then hurried off to telephone his and Wanda's families.

For a long time after Hank had left, Logan stood looking down at the child. Covertly watching him, Rachel noted that his jaw had hardened and his expression had become shuttered. "Hank's a lucky man," he said, abruptly breaking the silence. In the next moment, his manner became brisk. "Guess we'd better be getting back to the ranch. Wanda's not going to be up to having visitors for a while. We'll come back tomorrow to see her." Without giving Rachel a chance to respond, he strode off in search of Hank.

Rachel paused for one last look at the baby, then followed Logan.

"Wanda's family are on their way over," Hank said when they found him by the phones. He was grinning like a kid at Christmas.

"Then you'll have plenty of company," Logan replied. "Rachel and I are going back to the ranch now, but we'll be back to see Wanda and the baby again tomorrow."

"Sure thing," Hank replied. He glanced down the hall, obviously anxious to get back to his new son. "I'll see you tomorrow." And with that he headed off in the direction of the nursery.

Flying back to the ranch with Logan, Rachel felt herself growing tense. This time it would be just the two of them. *What difference does that make?* she ridiculed herself. It had been only the two of them in that house day and night for weeks. She glanced at Logan. It was his reticence that had her nerves on edge, she decided. He'd barely said a word since they'd left the hospital.

As he landed the helicopter beside the house, she again experienced a sense of homecoming. *You've got to stop thinking of this place in that way,* she warned herself.

Darkness had fallen. Her stomach growled as she climbed out of the helicopter, and she realized that neither she nor Logan had eaten since breakfast.

"I'll make some dinner for us," she said as they headed toward the house.

"While you do that, I'll check on the stock," he replied, tossing his keys on the hall table. He continued on through the house and out the kitchen door.

Rachel was just starting to make some roast-beef sandwiches, when the intercom from the stables clicked on.

"I need your help. Get down here fast," Logan ordered from the other end of the line.

Almost before his words were out, she was on her way. Panic caused her to run. Panting, she entered the stables to find him standing at the sink at the far end. His sleeves were rolled high on his arms and he was washing all the way to his elbows.

"Must be something in the air today," he said tersely. "Miss Rita's decided to give birth, too."

"Shall I call the vet?" Rachel asked, glancing worriedly toward the mare's stall.

Logan shook his head. "No time. We're going to have to do this ourselves."

A fresh rush of panic swept through her. "We?"

"You just do what I tell you," he said, passing her and entering the mare's stall.

Rachel followed him inside. Miss Rita was lying down.

"Talk to her soothingly," Logan instructed. "And stroke her neck. It'll help her relax."

Rachel knelt beside the horse's head. "Has it ever occurred to you that she might not want someone talking to her or stroking her at a time like this?" she asked Logan as she gently ran her hand down the horse's neck. In contrast to the skepticism in her words, she kept her voice soothing. "And I don't think anything I say or do is going to help her relax."

"You could be right," he admitted. "I've heard that at about this point in labor a lot of women begin to threaten their husbands with serious injury if they ever touch them again."

His attempt at humor helped ease Rachel's panic. "I've heard that, too," she confessed.

Miss Rita's nostrils were flared and she was breathing more rapidly. Rachel looked down at her sympathetically. "Everything will be all right," she assured the animal. "I may not be much help. But Logan knows what he's doing."

"I appreciate your confidence in me," Logan said. "But it looks as if we might be in for some trouble. The foal's coming out breech. I'm going to have to try to turn him."

Rachel's panic came back full force.

"I want you to put your hands on her stomach and tell me when you feel a contraction," he instructed. "The muscles will get hard like a rock."

Following his directions, Rachel spread her hands over the horse's belly. "I can feel the muscles tightening now," she said. Her own abdomen seemed to tighten in sympathy.

For the next half hour she watched Logan work. In the end, his arms, shirt and jeans were covered with blood, but a live foal emerged into the world.

"He's adorable," Rachel said, then flushed when she realized she'd used the same word to describe Wanda's baby only a few hours earlier.

"He's a she," Logan corrected, his attention quickly returning to the mare. "Push on her stomach," he ordered Rachel. "We still have the afterbirth to get out."

For the next few minutes they continued working with Miss Rita. To her relief, Rachel was certain the mare seemed more comfortable.

"Everything looks good," Logan announced finally. He made a final examination of Miss Rita and the foal, then nodded with approval. "Don't think there's any reason to call the vet and have him come over tonight. He can check them over later."

Rachel had been watching the foal try to stand. Reaching over, she patted her gently. "You'll get your balance soon," she assured her.

"It always takes a little while for them to find their feet," Logan said. He got up and stretched his sore muscles, then stood looking at her. "You were a big help. We worked well together."

The compliment brought a blush to her cheeks. "I'm glad I could assist," she replied. Again her eyes traveled to the foal. "It was exciting. Sort of like participating in a miracle."

"Sort of," he agreed. For a moment longer he stood there also watching the new foal, then said, "I don't know about you, but I'm starving. How about if we wash up and have that dinner now?"

Rachel's stomach growled as if to second this suggestion, and she got to her feet. "Sounds like a great idea to me."

Logan was already on his way to the sink at the end of the stable. "I'll just wash off some here, then take a quick shower at the house," he said over his shoulder.

Rachel leaned down to give the mare a final pat. "You've got a lovely daughter, Miss Rita," she said. Then straightening, she headed for the house.

She quickly bathed and dressed, then headed for the kitchen. Passing Logan's room, she heard his shower running. An image of him standing under the water as it cascaded over his muscular arms and shoulders suddenly filled her mind. Her blood seemed to warm and an excitement swept through her. "You really do need to control your fantasies," she chided herself and hurried on to make them some dinner.

She had the coffee perking and their salad and roast-beef sandwiches made when Logan entered.

There was a reserved air about him as he seated himself at the table. "I want to thank you again for your help," he said.

Rachel smiled softly at the memory of the new-born foal. "I honestly enjoyed it," she replied as she carried their cups of coffee to the table.

"Do you think after what you've seen today that you'd still consider having a child?" he asked, as she sat down across the table from him.

The sudden thought of having Logan's baby crossed her mind. Startled by how much she liked that idea, she shifted her gaze to her plate. *That wasn't what he'd asked,* she admonished herself. *He was merely making conversation.* However, he did expect an answer. "Yes," she replied honestly. "I'm sure both Wanda and Miss Rita would agree that the end result was worth the pain."

He acknowledged her answer with a nod, then concentrated on his food. Rachel did likewise. She was famished after this long day.

When they finished their sandwiches and salad, she asked him if he wanted a piece of apple pie for dessert, and he accepted with a nod. While she sliced the pie, he rose from the table and poured them both another cup of coffee. Catching a glimpse of him out of the corner of her eye, Rachel realized for the first time how much they had adapted to each other's habits. She'd been leaving the table to slice the pie even as she asked him if he wanted it. She'd known that he would. For his part, he hadn't even asked her if she wanted more coffee. He'd known she would.

Glancing out the window, she saw Hank and Wanda's darkened house. It was as if she and Logan were in a private world all their own, and she liked that feeling of togetherness. She chewed her bottom lip. That was why she'd been so tense on the flight back. She hadn't been worried about being alone with Logan, she'd been worried about liking it too much. This was *his* private world, she reminded herself. She was only a guest.

Carrying the plates of pie back to the table, she put them down, then seated herself. She noticed that Logan looked pensive as he picked up his fork. He'd been more reticent than usual during dinner, but she'd attributed that to tiredness and hunger. Now she wondered if he was worried about Miss Rita's foal. She was about to ask when he broke his silence.

"I've been thinking," he said, setting his fork aside and facing her levelly. "I've been thinking that Justin was right about one thing. It's time I got married and began producing heirs."

The food Rachel had just eaten suddenly felt like a lump of clay in her stomach. She'd agreed to be his friend, but she didn't want to be his confidante where affairs of the heart were concerned. She didn't want to hear that he had some woman he was considering as a wife, and she most certainly didn't want him telling her about how he was planning to propose, or even worse, asking her advice about how to go about proposing. But how could she refuse without revealing herself? *Maybe hearing about his plans will help get rid of these ridiculous fantasies I've been having,* she reasoned hopefully. Unable to face him, she concentrated on her pie. "I suppose if you do want children, now would be as good a time as any to get started."

"Part of the reason I've never married is that this place is a little too isolated for most people," he continued evenly. "It seems especially hard on women. But you don't seem to be bothered by it..." This last statement came out sounding like a question and he paused, as if waiting for an answer.

"No, it doesn't bother me." But to herself she admitted that he was the main reason the isolation didn't bother her. She simply liked being near him. She swallowed the lump that had suddenly formed in her throat and forced herself to add, "And I'm sure you can find a woman who'll suit you as a wife whom the isolation doesn't bother, either." *But I'm not going to stick around as the housekeeper,* she promised herself. If she could leave tonight, she would. She'd known this might happen, but she hadn't realized how difficult it would be.

"Truth is, I have someone in mind."

Rachel felt the bile rise in her throat. *What I feel for him is just physical. As soon as I leave this place, I'll forget him.*

"I've been thinking that we get along well together," he was saying. "We've gotten used to each other's habits without any real trouble and don't seem to get on each other's nerves. We work well together, too. Miss Rita's delivery could have gone badly today if you hadn't been there. I'm not going to promise to change my life-style. We'd go on pretty much the same as we are now. But I can guarantee that no matter how things work out in the end, I'd make certain you're financially secure for the rest of your life.''

Rachel stared at him. His jaw was tensed and his shoulders squared as if he was making a business presentation. ''Anyway,'' he continued gruffly, ''it seems to me that we would make a reasonable couple. We could, at least, give it a try.''

Rachel couldn't believe what she was hearing. She wanted to, but was afraid. ''Are you propositioning me, or are you proposing?'' she finally asked.

''I want heirs, not bastards,'' he growled. He scowled self-consciously. ''Guess I should have realized you'd think of this as a joke.'' Abruptly he pushed his chair back from the table and rose.

Rachel was on her feet in the same instant. ''I don't. I didn't mean it that way.'' She felt as if her whole life hung in the balance as she met his gaze. ''I honestly wasn't certain what you were leading up to. It never occurred me that you'd consider marrying me.''

He stood stiffly, watching her. ''We get along well. We like a lot of the same things. Seems to me like a logical thing for me to do.''

Married to Logan. Even in her fantasies, she'd never let herself go that far. Agreement was on the tip of her tongue, but sudden doubts assailed her. "You're talking about an intimate relationship," she said shakily. "I'm not a brood mare. I'd have to feel there was some attraction, some passion between us, even if it was only physical."

Logan regarded her dryly. "I suppose that's a polite way of saying that I'm not your type. Well, you can't hold it against a man for asking." He started toward the door. "I'd better go check on Miss Rita."

"It was *me* being *your* type I was asking about," she blurted out. Pride brought her voice back to a more even keel. "I wouldn't like to think that you'd have to pretend I was someone else before your passion was aroused." *Idiot!* she chided herself. *You should have let him go. Not only are you making a fool of yourself, this marriage he's proposing can't last.*

He turned back toward her. His eyes darkened as his gaze traveled over her. "I wouldn't have to do any pretending. The truth is it hasn't been easy for me these past weeks with you here. After all, I am a normal, red-blooded male, and you're one hell of an appealing female."

Heat traveled from the tips of her toes to the top of her head. "In that case, I suppose we could give it a try," she said, trying to sound nonchalant while her heart was pounding so fast and hard she could barely get her breath.

"Good," he replied with finality. "Tomorrow you can have the blood test done when we go to the hospital to see Wanda."

"What about you?"

He smiled sheepishly. "In Montana men don't have to have a blood test."

She rewarded him with a disgruntled grimace. "Lucky you."

He grinned, then his manner became business-like again. "Do you have anyone you want to invite to the wedding?"

She shook her head. "No one."

"Then after I've checked on Miss Rita," he said, "I'll call my mother and stepfather. I figured we'd get married the day after tomorrow. No sense in waiting now that the decision's been made. If they can make it by then, fine. If not, they'll just have to miss the wedding."

Rachel was a little surprised by his hurry to get the wedding over with. *Maybe he's worried that if he gives himself time to think about it, he'll change his mind,* she thought anxiously. "Are you sure you want to rush into this so quickly?" she asked, watching him closely for any sign of hesitation.

He traced the line of her jaw with his thumb. "I'm sure."

The feel of his touch and the way he was looking at her made any kind of rational thinking impossible. "In that case, whatever arrangements you want to make are fine with me," she said, marveling at her ability to put together a coherent sentence.

He smiled. "I'm glad to hear that. And now to seal our bargain."

His hands cupped her face and he lowered his head toward hers. He began the kiss gently.

Wondering what it would feel like to be kissed by him was nothing compared to the real thing, Rachel thought as the taste of him awoke desire. When he nibbled gently on her lower lip, currents of excitement shot through her. Not even realizing what she was doing, she reached up and lightly caressed his jaw, then let her hands travel to the strong cords at the back of his neck.

"You *are* a temptation," he murmured against her skin. Then deepening the kiss, he wound his arms around her and drew her close.

He's just been very lonely out here by himself, she told herself. *I'll be nothing more than a warm body to him.* But she didn't care. He was igniting a fire that was like nothing she'd ever felt before and it was too delicious a sensation to resist.

Then abruptly he released her. "Keeping my hands off you for another two days is going to be one heck of a strain on my willpower," he said in a low growl. Again he traced the line of her jaw with his thumb, then, quickly placing a final, feather-light kiss on her lips, walked out of the room.

Standing numbly, her legs feeling like jelly, Rachel muttered, "At least I don't have to worry about any lack of passion."

Chapter Nine

"I've been wondering what Logan's been so preoccupied about these past weeks," Hank said with a wide grin.

It was the next day and they were in Wanda's hospital room. Logan, with Rachel at his side, had just told Wanda and Hank about his and Rachel's impending marriage.

Wanda smiled at Rachel. "I had noticed you getting a certain look in your eye whenever Logan's name was mentioned," she said with a nod. "I should have guessed there was something going on between the two of you."

Rachel glanced at Logan. She hoped he wasn't taking what Wanda said seriously. Her instinct for survival cautioned her that it would not be wise for him to guess how attracted she was to him. Besides, it's only physical, she assured herself once again. She'd probably even get bored with him after a while—before, she hoped, he got bored with her. Again she questioned the wisdom of entering a marriage she felt certain couldn't last. Then he put his arm around her waist and just his touch caused a flame of desire within her.

"It's nice to have a couple of romantics around," Logan said as he and Rachel left the hospital a little while later. His tone indicated that he found the inferences Hank and Wanda had made about him and Rachel being in love ridiculous. But there was also relief in his voice.

Rachel knew that Logan's interest in her was purely physical, and she was glad he hadn't taken what Wanda had said seriously. But the relief in his voice brought back a nagging anxiety she'd been trying to ignore since the night before. It had begun after Logan called his mother to tell her about the marriage and invite her to the wedding.

"My mother and stepfather will be coming to the wedding," he'd informed her. "We'll pick them up at the airport and go directly from there to the courthouse to get our license. I figured we'd get married right there by the justice of the peace—unless you prefer to find a minister."

"The courthouse is fine with me," she'd replied. His manner was nonchalant, but she'd detected a guardedness beneath the surface and she'd never been one to turn away from the truth. "How did your mother take the news?" she'd asked bluntly.

"She was a little surprised, but she sends her congratulations," he'd replied. Then before she could ask any more questions, he'd said it had been a long day and he thought they should both go to bed and get some rest. Then he'd bidden her a quick good-night and gone to his room.

She'd been tempted to follow him and challenge his statement that his mother had sent her congratulations, but she hadn't. It was a fool's dream... living here on a ranch forever with Logan, having his children...having him learn to honestly care for her. But what harm could there be in living with the fantasy for one night?

However, the night was over, it was now the next day. She had a bandage on her arm where the nurse had drawn blood. *You have to ask him about his mother,* she ordered herself. *You've got to know now if he's having second thoughts before this goes any further.* "I've had a feeling that you weren't entirely honest with me about your mother's reaction," she said as they left the hospital.

He shrugged. "My mother does not make my decisions."

Rachel had always envied people with close families. She'd always longed to be a part of one and would never do anything to tear one apart. "I wouldn't want to cause any trouble between you and your mother,'' she said tightly.

"You won't," he assured her. Abruptly he halted and turned to face her. His gaze narrowed. "Rachel, I want the truth. Is it really my mother you're worried about, or are you having second thoughts?"

"I thought maybe you were," she replied.

He traced the line of her jaw with the tip of his finger. "No, I'm not. But if you want out, I want to know now."

His touch had left a trail of fire. *You're only asking for trouble if you go through with this,* her inner voice warned. But she paid it no heed. "No, I don't want out," she said.

He smiled then, and the warmth in his eyes made her toes curl. "Good," he said, then tucking her arm through his, he continued toward their rented car.

As they drove away from the hospital, Rachel drew a shaky breath. This wasn't a traditional marriage, but it would still have a "wedding night!" And she wanted something special to wear. At least, something a little sexier than what she currently owned.

Her stomach felt as if butterflies were in there. She'd always kept barriers between herself and others, and thus, her experience with men was extremely limited. *I definitely need something to boost my confidence,* she decided. "I'd like to do a little private shopping," she said as they drove away from the hospital.

"Sure thing," Logan replied. "I've got a few errands I want to run myself. But first there's the matter of wedding rings."

At the jewelry store, Logan insisted on buying her an engagement ring, as well. Rachel tried to refuse and told him it wasn't necessary. But Logan was insistent. "I want to do this right," he said, and from the set of his jaw she knew that arguing would be futile. She did, however, choose a more modest stone than the one he first picked out.

"I don't want people thinking that I'm marrying you for your money," she said.

"Nope, wouldn't want that," he replied with a grin and a wink for the jeweler who was showing them the rings.

But Rachel noticed that the grin didn't reach his eyes, and she wished she'd kept her mouth shut. It might have been better to let him think that she *was* doing this for mercenary reasons. Fervently she hoped he would let the remark pass. But her hopes weren't answered.

"I was wondering," Logan said in his easy drawl as they left the store. "Just why *are* you marrying me if it isn't for the security my money can give you?"

A strong rush of fear surged through her. She'd learned to protect herself from the world by never allowing her true feelings to show. And in this instance, hiding them was especially important. This attraction she had for him made her feel frighteningly vulnerable. Again she told herself that it was merely physical and would fade in time, but at the moment it was incredibly powerful. "I didn't say it wasn't for the security. I merely said I didn't want people saying I was marrying you for your money," she replied, managing to keep her tone light.

He shrugged as if to say her reasons were of no real consequence to him. "I figured that was probably the case," he said and, to her relief, let the subject drop.

They parted company soon after that.

A little later, Rachel was glaring at herself in the mirror of the dressing room in a lingerie shop. Picking out a nightgown had become one of the most difficult decisions she'd ever made. "I don't know what you're worried about," she muttered to the image in the mirror. "It's not as if it really matters what you wear. This isn't a traditional marriage. It's more of a business deal." This thought, instead of making her feel more relaxed, only served to increase the tension in her muscles. What if Logan turned out to be a real disappointment as a lover?

"Then this attraction I feel will vanish and I'll be able to leave him and his ranch without a backward glance," was her response. In fact, it might even be better if that was the case, she reasoned as she left the store with her purchases. It unnerved her the way he'd become such an important part of her existence. Before he'd come into her life, she'd been totally independent. Now it was as if she wasn't totally complete unless he was near. "You've got to get over this," she warned herself, "or you're going to get hurt."

During the flight back to the ranch, she worked on strengthening her wall of reserve against him, but failed miserably. There was always a distraction. She'd catch a glimpse of his jaw, and the urge to run her finger along its hard contours would surge through her. A couple of times a ray from the sun caught her ring and she saw herself beside him in front of the justice of the peace. This image caused both fear and excitement to sweep through her. Maybe this marriage wasn't such a good idea, she cautioned herself for the hundredth time. But she couldn't make herself suggest they call it off.

As the ranch house came into sight, he nodded toward the ground. "Looks like we've got company."

Rachel looked down and saw the blue coupe parked in front of the house. "Is it the vet?" she asked, knowing Logan had called him and asked him to come by to check that everything was all right with Miss Rita and her foal.

"Not unless he's got a new car," Logan replied, scowling.

Rachel had the feeling he'd guessed who was there and wasn't happy about it. She was about to ask when her question was answered by the visitors' coming out onto the porch and waving. The woman was Logan's mother. Beside her was a tall, medium-built man with gray hair. The tailored slacks and pullover shirt he wore made him look as if he'd just stepped off a golf course at an exclusive country club. Logan's stepfather, she decided.

She was right.

"I hope you don't mind our coming early," Gail McGreggor said as Logan and Rachel joined them on the porch. "Since we'll be leaving right after the wedding so that the two of you can have your privacy, it didn't seem reasonable to fly all the way to Billings just for a few hours tomorrow. So we thought we'd come today and that would give us an evening together. I thought George and Rachel should have a little time to get to know one another."

In spite of her attempt to appear casual, the way Logan's mother rattled on made it clear she was nervous. Rachel was certain the McGreggors were there for a purpose. Most likely to try to talk Logan out of this marriage, she concluded. Well, she couldn't blame them. Maybe it would be just as well if they succeeded, her reasonable side conceded. But the thought caused her stomach to twist painfully. If they did succeed, she would use the opportunity to leave, she promised herself, because where Logan was concerned her emotions were totally out of control. "I'll go fix us some dinner," she said with false cheerfulness, looking for an opportunity to escape.

"And I'll help." Gail gave her husband an encouraging smile. "That will give us time to visit and the men a chance to be by themselves."

So she was going to let her husband try to talk some sense into Logan, Rachel mused cynically. A few minutes later, as she left her room where she'd put her packages and changed into a pair of jeans, she noticed that the door to Logan's study was closed. Could be all that worrying she'd done about negligees might have been for nothing, she thought, trying to come to terms with the possibility of the wedding being canceled. But her stomach only twisted more. *You know it'd be for the best,* her inner voice admonished. But that didn't make it any easier. She'd never wanted anything as badly as she wanted to be Logan's wife, even for just a short while. Some wishes are nothing but trouble, she told herself curtly and hurried into the kitchen.

"I thought maybe we could make something simple like omelets," Gail suggested, practically jumping up from her chair as Rachel entered.

Obviously whatever was going on between the two men in the study had Logan's mother painfully nervous, Rachel observed. She felt sorry for the woman, but she wasn't certain what she could say or do to alleviate Mrs. McGreggor's anxiety. For now it might be best to play it cool, she decided. "Omelets sound fine," she agreed. "I'll make some biscuits while you cut up whatever you think might make good fillings.''

Gail was on her way to the refrigerator even before Rachel had finished speaking.

"Why don't you tell me about Logan's brothers and sisters,'' Rachel suggested as she began to measure out ingredients and Gail began slicing onions. She hoped that talking would ease the woman's tenseness.

Gail looked relieved to have something to occupy her mind other than the two men down the hall. In the same sort of rattling voice she'd used on the porch, she began to give Rachel details about Logan's half siblings and their children.

It was a large family, larger than Rachel had imagined, and the love in Gail's voice suggested it was also a close family.

"All of his nieces and nephews adore Logan,'' Gail was saying as she finished dicing the red and green peppers and started on the tomatoes. There was a gentleness in her voice as if she was picturing the children gathered around the tall cowboy.

The same sort of picture formed in Rachel's mind, and a smile played at the corners of her mouth.

Suddenly the kitchen door opened and Logan strode in. "I've got to go check on Miss Rita,'' he growled, barely glancing at either of the women as he grabbed his coat and left by the back door.

George entered the kitchen just as Logan left. Approaching Gail, he shook his head in a manner that indicated his mission had failed. "It might be best if we drove back into town and spent the night there," he said. Turning toward Rachel, he smiled apologetically. "We shouldn't have intruded. Tell Logan we'll meet you at the courthouse tomorrow."

Gail looked pleadingly at her husband. "He did understand we weren't trying to cause any trouble?" she said anxiously, her voice barely above a whisper.

"I think it might be best if we left," George repeated, slipping an arm around his wife's waist. "We can talk on the drive back to Billings." As he guided Gail toward the kitchen door, he paused to look at Rachel. "It was nice to meet you," he said in the same polite tones he'd used a moment ago. "We'll be looking forward to the wedding tomorrow."

As a convicted felon looks forward to the electric chair, Rachel thought cynically. "Wait," she requested. She knew she wasn't going to like what she would hear, but she'd never been one to turn away from reality no matter how unpleasant. Besides, this wasn't going to go away. Whatever the problem was, if she married Logan, she would have to face it sooner or later. "I'm not stupid. Logan was obviously angry, and you two are planning a hasty retreat. And I'm certain I'm the cause. I would never have agreed to marry Logan if I thought it was going to cause trouble between him and his family. I would appreciate it if you would tell me exactly what is going on." Her body stiffened as if she was preparing for a blow she wanted to take without flinching, no matter how much it hurt. "Do you object to his marrying me because I have a police record?"

"No, no." Gail shook her head to emphasize her denial. "We understand the circumstances behind your arrest. You were young and scared."

"You should have been sent to a foster home, not to jail," George added.

They seemed so sincere Rachel believed them. Still, she was certain they had come to stop the marriage. "But you object to my marrying him," she persisted, determined not to shy away from the truth.

"No, we don't object to your marrying him," Gail assured her.

George's manner became that of the very successful lawyer he was. "It's just that in this day and age, marriages seem to be so unstable, and, let's be honest, Logan is a wealthy man. We simply thought it might be prudent if the two of you signed a prenuptial agreement."

Gail glared at her husband. "I really don't think it's necessary for Rachel to be bothered with this, George, since Logan has obviously rejected the suggestion."

Rachel saw the fear behind the anger in Gail's eyes. She either thinks I'll use this to try to turn Logan against them or I'll hate them for trying to interfere, she realized.

"She's most likely going to find out why we were here, anyway," George replied to his wife in reasoning tones.

Gail rewarded this statement with a scowl. Then, her expression taking on a pleading quality, she turned her attention to Rachel. "It's not as if we think you're marrying Logan for his money," she explained hurriedly. "He's much too smart to let a woman do that."

At least you hope he is, Rachel added to herself, catching the doubt in Gail's voice. Their distrust hurt, but she refused to allow that to show. "I've heard that prenuptial agreements are in vogue these days," she said with casual nonchalance. It suddenly occurred to her that maybe she was taking all of this too personally. "I suppose you've counseled all your children to have these documents drawn up before they married."

Gail flashed a questioning glance at George, and Rachel had her answer. They hadn't made this suggestion to any of their other children, but Logan's mother was wondering if she should lie and say that they had.

"None of our other children have Logan's kind of wealth," George replied.

George's calm expression was slipping, and Rachel read the growing uneasiness in his eyes. They were both very worried about the effect she was going to have on their relationship with Logan. It was painful that they were questioning her motives, but then, why should they trust her? They didn't know her. Besides, she should be used to having to earn people's trust by now. More importantly, they hadn't lied to her, and she couldn't fault them for caring about Logan. She gave a shrug as if her last question was unimportant. "Actually, if I was in your shoes, I'd have suggested a prenuptial agreement, too. It sounds quite sensible to me." She forced a polite smile and extended a hand toward George. "Although I'm sure it's fair, I would like to read it before I sign it."

For a moment shock registered on their faces, then was replaced by relief.

"It's very equitable," George assured her. "Logan refused to consider it, but I left it on his desk, anyway."

"I'll just go read it," Rachel said, glad of an excuse to be alone. Walking down the hall to Logan's study, she tried to ignore the hard knot in her stomach. It shouldn't hurt that Logan's parents were suspicious of her motives. They were right in their guess that this wasn't a marriage based on love. "It's simply a practical arrangement, and a prenuptial agreement fits in perfectly," she muttered to herself as she seated herself at Logan's desk and began to read.

George hadn't lied to her. Her share, if the marriage was dissolved, was more than fair. But she had no intention of taking anything from Logan.

Carrying the agreement with her, she returned to the kitchen. George was sitting at the table worriedly watching his wife pace.

"I knew we shouldn't have come here," Gail was saying anxiously. "Logan's just like his father when it comes to making decisions. He's bullheaded and stubborn. And he doesn't like having his choices questioned."

"I've read the document," Rachel said, letting them know that she had returned.

Gail gave a start, while George rose to his feet with dignity. "And what do you think of it?" he asked.

"You're right. It's more than fair," she replied. "But I'd like it reworked to say that what is Logan's remains Logan's and what is mine remains mine."

Gail looked stricken. "I really don't think it's necessary to go that far."

"It's what I want," Rachel insisted. Her gaze leveled on George. "Would you do that for me this evening after dinner?" Her jaw hardened with purpose. "It's much too late for the two of you to drive back into Billings. And I really would like for you to stay."

"Would he do what for you?"

All three had been so absorbed in their own conversation none had heard the back door open. Now they jerked around to see that Logan had entered the kitchen.

There was a threat in the rancher's eyes as he looked at his stepfather.

"I've asked him to make some adjustments to our prenuptial agreement," Rachel replied quickly before Logan could say anything he might later regret.

Logan's gaze shifted to her. The threat was replaced by a cynical glimmer. "So you think a prenuptial agreement is a good idea?"

She stiffened. He thought she wanted to ensure she'd be entitled to some of his wealth. She read it in his eyes. Well, why shouldn't he? That had been a part of his proposal. And today she'd practically told him she was marrying him for his money.

"She wants me to draw up an agreement that states simply that what is yours now remains yours and what is hers remains hers," George elaborated. "I tried to explain to her that this agreement I've drawn up is quite fair and reasonable."

Logan's expression became shuttered. Striding across the room, he caught Rachel by the arm. "You and I need to have a little talk," he said, already guiding her out of the kitchen and into the corridor.

"I don't understand what we have to talk about," she protested, trying to pull free before they reached his study. She didn't want to have to explain her actions to him. She was too afraid of what she might reveal. "We've agreed to a marriage based on practicality. A prenuptial agreement seemed like a reasonable addition."

He made no response.

His silence unnerved her. She glanced up at the hard set of his jaw. Maybe he had decided that it would be best to call the wedding off. She ignored the sharp jab of disappointment this thought caused.

When they reached his study, he guided her inside. There he released her arm, then closed the door and locked it. Once their privacy was ensured, he turned back to face her. "I want to know why the hell you're marrying me, Rachel. I assumed it was for the security my money would give you. This morning you practically admitted that was your only reason. Now you want George to draw up a prenuptial agreement that leaves you with nothing but what you have now. I'd feel a lot more secure if I knew what your real motives were."

Lying wasn't working. She kept getting caught. Drawing a shaky breath, she settled for a portion of the truth. "I like it here. I feel comfortable here. You and I get along. I've always wanted a family and a place where I can feel like I really belong.

Marriage to you seemed like a good way to achieve that."

He suddenly smiled that easy smile of his. "I have to admit I like that explanation a lot better than thinking that the security my money can provide was the only reason you were marrying me. That was a little hard on my ego, and I was having some doubts about the longevity of a marriage based on mercenary motives." Then the smile vanished. "But no matter how practical or sincere our motives are, things may not work out for us, and in that case I intend to see that you have financial security. That was part of the deal I offered you."

Deal. Bargain. Contract. Mutually beneficial alliance. That was what this marriage was to him. *And that's what it is to me, and I must never think that it can be anything more,* she ordered herself. Still, she had her pride. Besides, she had never intended to gain financially by this alliance. "I have money I've saved. If this marriage doesn't work out, I can take care of myself."

He shook his head at her stubbornness. "Is it so difficult for you to accept help from someone?"

Her mind flashed back to a few minutes earlier in the kitchen. "Help" hadn't been what she'd seen in Logan's eyes when George had said she wanted to alter the already drawn-up agreement. It had been cynical suspicion. She could accept his parents' concern, but to have Logan think for even a moment that she would consider trying to take a huge hunk of his wealth had hurt more than she wanted to admit. "What is difficult for me," she said tersely, "is always having to prove myself to people. To prove that my intentions are not evil and I'm not out to cause anyone any harm." Her jaw hardened with a resolve equal to his. "A prenuptial agreement will put everyone's mind at ease and I intend to have one. And I want it drawn up my way!"

For a long moment he regarded her in silence, then he shrugged. "You can have your agreement, but it will be the one George has already drawn up."

A refusal formed but she held it back. She knew from the expression on Logan's face that arguing would do no good. Besides, she could always refuse to take anything. "Fine," she said.

Returning to the kitchen, they found George again sitting at the table. This time he was drumming his fingers on the table while his wife paced.

Seeing Logan and Rachel enter, Gail rushed toward them. "We didn't come here to cause trouble," she said, capturing Rachel's hand and giving it a reassuring squeeze. "Really, we have no objections to your marrying Logan." Still holding Rachel's hand, her gaze swung to her son. "Please don't be angry with us."

"Neither of us is angry with you," Rachel assured her. Her attention turned to George. "Logan has convinced me that it will be less trouble for everyone if I sign the paper you have already drawn up.''

''I didn't come here to force anyone to sign anything,'' George said, his tone suggesting that he wished he hadn't even broached the subject of a prenuptial agreement.

''You're not forcing anyone,'' she replied. ''Now, how about if I get that thing signed and we get on with dinner. I'm starved.''

Gail's hold on Rachel's hand tightened. ''Are you certain this is what you want? We really shouldn't have interfered.''

''I'm certain,'' Rachel replied, gently freeing her hand and moving toward the table where George's briefcase sat.

''The signing will have to wait until tomorrow,'' George said. ''We'll need witnesses.''

Rachel shrugged as if it made no difference to her when or where it was signed. ''Fine. Then I'm going to get busy and finish making the biscuits.''

Taking her cue from Rachel, Gail busied herself with the ingredients for the omelets. Logan insisted on setting the table and George hovered in the background. The tension in the kitchen was so thick it could have been cut with a knife.

Hoping to alleviate it, Rachel began asking Gail questions about her grandchildren. Logan contributed a couple of anecdotes. The tension didn't totally subside, but it eased. However, by the time the dishes were cleared, Rachel was exhausted from the strain of putting up a cheerful, nonchalant facade. She guessed the others were, too.

As soon as she could, Rachel pleaded tiredness and escaped to her room. When they wished her a good-night, Gail and George both told her they were happy for her and Logan. But in spite of their assurances, she still felt like an outsider.

Snuggling under her covers, she lay staring into the dark. She hadn't lied about being tired, but sleep refused to come as doubts again assailed her. If Logan was marrying her because he loved her, it would be different. But he didn't love her. Nevertheless, she didn't want to leave. She wanted to be Logan's wife.

"And it could last. We have as good a chance as any other couple," she affirmed in hushed tones, needing to hear herself say it aloud, hoping that would give her words more validity. "We're used to one another. We've got no illusions about ourselves. I'll be a good wife to him. It can work." Her jaw formed a determined line. "It *will* work."

Chapter Ten

The next morning, Gail and George ate a quick breakfast, then left to drive to Billings.

Logan had arranged for Jed Marshal to help with the chores for the next few days. Jed had a small ranch a few miles down the road and worked as a part-time hand for Logan during particularly busy times, or when Logan or Hank was away.

As soon as his mother and stepfather had left, Logan went out to give Jed orders and to check on a few things himself.

Alone in the kitchen, Rachel washed up the dishes and fought back a fresh surge of doubts. Then she saw Logan returning to the house. Her pulse quickened and she felt a rush of excitement.

She knew it wasn't smart, but she couldn't make herself give up this opportunity to be with him.

The hospital was Rachel and Logan's first stop when they reached Billings. After picking up the documentation they needed for the license, they went up to see Wanda and the baby for a few minutes.

"I don't think I've ever seen Logan nervous," Wanda said in hushed tones to Rachel as the cowboy crossed to the window while the two women cooed to the baby. There was a twinkle of amusement in Wanda's eyes.

But Rachel wasn't amused. She'd noticed Logan's nervousness as they'd driven to the hospital, and she was again beginning to wonder if he'd changed his mind about the wedding.

When they left the hospital a few minutes later and began walking toward their rented car, she decided to give him one last chance to back out. "I've been wondering if you're having second thoughts," she said carefully, bracing herself for him to admit that he was.

He glanced at her. "Not me. But I've been worried about you. Every once in a while I see a pensive expression come over your face." He stopped and placed his hands on her shoulders, holding her squarely in front of him. "I think we've got a good chance to make this marriage work as long as we're both committed to giving it our best try."

She met his steady gaze. "I want it to work," she admitted honestly.

He smiled. "Good. Then let's get going."

George and Gail arrived at the courthouse soon after Logan and Rachel had obtained the license.

"The justice of the peace is an old family friend," Logan explained as he led the way through the courthouse. "We can use his chambers for signing the agreement. He's in court right now, but the noon recess will begin soon and he'll marry us then."

They had just reached the doors of the judge's chambers when a familiar voice called out from behind them. Turning, Rachel saw Hank approaching with the baby in one arm and Wanda holding on to the other.

"You didn't think we'd let Logan get married without being here, did you?" Hank demanded with a laugh.

"The baby and I came for Rachel," Wanda added, giving Rachel a hug.

"I'm glad you're here," Rachel said, returning Wanda's hug. For the first time in a long time, she felt as if she had real friends, and happiness bubbled up inside of her.

"We just have one small errand to take care of before the wedding," Logan was saying as he greeted Hank with a handshake. Opening the doors of the judge's chambers, he motioned for everyone to enter.

Once inside, George opened his briefcase and took out the agreement.

"If you two don't mind witnessing this, it'll save me the trouble of finding someone," Logan requested.

Hank shook his head. "I always knew you were a careful man about keeping your affairs in order. Got yourself a new will drawn up already, huh?"

Logan frowned impatiently at the document as if it was of little value. "It's not a new will. It's a prenuptial agreement. George and my mother thought it would be a good idea, and Rachel agreed."

"I don't want people thinking I'm marrying Logan for his money," Rachel quipped. Then she saw it—Wanda turned toward Hank with an "I told you so" smirk on her face. It was only a momentary glance, but the joy Rachel had been feeling faded. Obviously even Hank had had some questions about her motives. But Wanda hadn't, she pointed out to herself. One out of five was better than none.

Picking up the pen, she signed the document.

That had been the beginning of the most nerve-racking afternoon of Rachel's life. The wedding ceremony was over quickly, and immediately afterward Hank, Wanda and the baby had left for Wanda's parents' home. They'd be staying there for a couple of weeks before returning to the ranch.

George and Gail's plane to Los Angeles didn't leave until late afternoon. After Hank and Wanda's departure, they insisted on treating Logan and Rachel to a nice lunch. At first, Rachel had been relieved at not being suddenly alone with Logan. She told herself it was ridiculous to be apprehensive about their wedding night, but she was.

The meal, however, didn't help calm her. It seemed to drag on forever. Making small talk had never been one of her strong points. And worse, every time she looked at Logan, she remembered the feel of his lips when he'd kissed her after they'd been pronounced husband and wife, and a rush of heat went through her. It hadn't been a long kiss, or even a passionate one. After all, they'd had an audience. But there had been a possessiveness in the way the palms of his hands had flattened against her back when he'd held her, and a firmness in the way his lips had met hers. The contact had lasted only seconds, but it had sent a thrill coursing through her.

Finally the meal ended, they all said their goodbyes, and Logan and Rachel flew back to the ranch. During the flight, Rachel found herself glancing down several times at the gold band on her finger. She and Logan were married. It didn't seem real. She was glad the noise of the helicopter made talking difficult. All of a sudden she wasn't certain what to say to him.

Eventually she saw the ranch coming into view. Her heart began to pound faster as a fresh wave of nervousness washed over her.

"I'm sorry we couldn't get away for a proper honeymoon," he said a few minutes later as they left the helicopter and walked toward the house. "But until Hank can take over for me, I don't feel right about leaving. I suspect it'll take a couple of months for him to adjust to fatherhood. Until then, he won't be able to devote full time to the ranch."

"Actually I feel more comfortable starting our life here," Rachel replied, for the first time not having to remind herself not to think of this ranch as home. Now it *was* her home. Logan had draped his arm casually around her shoulders. She doubted he was even aware of the contact, but for her his touch made her have to fight the urge to move even closer to him.

As they reached the door, his hand tightened on her shoulder and he brought her to a halt. "I'm a man who believes in tradition," he said.

Suddenly she was scooped up in his arms and he carried her over the threshold and into the house. Pausing only to kick the door shut, he continued down the hall toward his room.

"I hope you don't feel I'm rushing you," he said huskily, "But having you here and keeping my distance has been a strain. And the way I caught you looking at me a couple of times during lunch didn't make waiting any easier."

Rachel's heart was now pounding furiously. The thought that she'd spent a lot of needless time worrying about what nightgown to wear flashed through her mind. A giggle tickled her throat. Realizing this was more nerves than humor, she swallowed it back.

She was acutely aware of the sturdy strength of the arms that cradled her. Every nerve in her body awakened with tingling excitement. The waiting hadn't been easy for her, either. Nevertheless, for one brief moment she was reluctant to let him know that she was just as anxious as he was. But as she shifted slightly to put her arms around his neck for a better hold, her breast brushed against the hard wall of his chest and a wave of desire so strong it caused her to tremble washed over her.

Logan came to an abrupt halt. "I didn't mean to frighten you," he said gruffly.

Be coy, she ordered herself. But she didn't feel like being coy. "I'm not frightened," she heard herself saying in a tone as husky as his.

The brown of his eyes darkened and he smiled. Then he continued down the hall.

Well, I never claimed I wasn't attracted to him, she reasoned, then again told herself that it was merely a physical thing. But one heck of a powerful physical thing, she conceded as they entered his bedroom.

Releasing her slowly so that her body remained close to his, he stood her on the floor in front of him. "I don't believe I have ever kissed you properly," he said, then claimed her mouth in a kiss that made up for any previous inadequacy.

Rachel's hands moved caressingly over his shoulders, then to the strong hard cords of his neck. Nothing in her whole life had ever felt this good.

He deserted her mouth and found her earlobe.

She gasped with pleasure as he gently took a light nip. Her blood was racing now. She had wondered what it would be like to be in his arms, but she'd never dreamed it could be this exciting. Her hands moved to the lapels of his suit coat and he loosened his hold to allow her to remove it.

A part of her felt wanton, then she reminded herself that she was his wife. There was no reason for her to deny herself pleasure. She discarded his tie and unbuttoned the top buttons of his shirt while he stood watching her.

Unable to resist, she paused to kiss the hollow of his neck.

His hands had been resting on her hips, now they moved lower and he pulled her against him. "You're having a detrimental effect on my patience," he warned.

A surge of womanly power like none she'd ever felt before caused a flush of delight. "I can tell," she murmured.

Laughing lightly, he freed her, then began removing her clothing. Rachel considered helping, but she was enjoying the delicious sensation his undressing her was creating too much to interfere. His touch spread fire and the look in his eyes as each layer came off only served to cause the fire of desire in her to burn hotter.

She had thought she would feel embarrassed to be standing naked in front of him, but instead, the look of passion in his eyes brought a warm glow of pleasure.

"Now it's my turn," she said, returning to unbuttoning his shirt.

After discarding that article of clothing, she began unbuckling his belt. Glancing up at him, she saw the slightly embarrassed flush creeping up his neck and an impishness brought a smile to her lips. "This is fun," she said, returning her concentration to the task at hand.

The strength of his body fascinated her. She paused to trace the line of an old scar that ran across his hard, flat abdomen.

"I did a little bull riding in the rodeos in my younger days," he said as if trying to concentrate on something other than her touch. "Had a close call with a pair of horns and gave it up."

"Obviously a serious disagreement," she qualified. Her finger again followed the line with a caressing touch. "I'm glad you gave it up."

"I try to use some common sense when it comes to flirting with danger." The brown of his eyes deepened to mahogany. "But I'm beginning to think I might have underestimated just how dangerous you could be."

The way he said it caused a fresh surge of womanly power to wash over her. She glanced up at him coquettishly. "Is that your way of saying that you're having second thoughts?"

"Second thoughts are not the kind I'm having," he replied.

Rachel laughed lightly. She'd expected to feel nervous, even a little frightened. But this was fun. Diligently she finished undressing him, then stood letting her gaze travel over him. Unable to resist she ran her hand along the length of his thigh.

"You do try a man's patience," he murmured huskily. Reaching down, he caught the covers on the bed and tossed them back. "I hope you're ready to consummate this marriage," he said as he picked her up and placed her on the sheets, "because I'm only a mere mortal and waiting another second is beyond my endurance."

Her mind blurred by the raging flames of passion, she could only nod as her hand moved exploringly over the strong musculature of his chest.

There was a momentary expression of surprise on his face as he claimed her.

Rachel gasped back a startled cry of pain. Then the instant of discomfort was forgotten as his touch soothed her and she was again aware only of the exhilarating sensations of desire.

Afterward, he held her snuggled up against him, her head resting on his shoulder. Rachel was acutely aware of him. There was a tenseness about him that puzzled her. She, herself, had never felt so relaxed or so contented.

"You should have warned me that you were inexperienced," he admonished, combing her thick black tresses off her cheek with his fingers. "I would have tried to be more gentle."

His touch was tantalizing as his fingers brushed her ear. "It was very nice as it was," she assured him lazily. "I really don't think you could have improved on your performance."

He laughed a soft relieved laugh and she felt his body relax.

She was shaken by the realization that he'd been honestly concerned that he might have hurt her. She wasn't used to anyone really caring about her. Closing her eyes, she wished she could hold on to this moment forever.

His hand moved along the curves of her body. "You're certain you've got no complaints?"

The playfulness in his voice brought a grin to her face. Levering herself up on an elbow, she gave him a mock, impatient scowl. "If you're looking for more compliments, you'll have to work for them." She was momentarily startled by her wanton banter, then she gave a mental shrug. Why shouldn't she enjoy this? She deserved to have as much fun in her life as anyone else. *As long as I don't let myself start counting on it lasting forever,* she cautioned herself.

"You are a threat to a man's stamina," he said in a low, teasing growl.

His hands began a slow, sensual, intimate exploration that quickly rekindled her desire. *But as long as it does last, I might as well enjoy myself thor-*

oughly, and, smiling softly, she kissed the hollow of his neck.

The problem, she decided a few weeks later, was that she was enjoying herself too much. She was standing at the kitchen sink watching him walk toward the house. It was lunchtime, but lunch wasn't what she had on her mind. His dusty, work-worn jeans fitted his muscular thighs snugly. He shifted his shoulders in a stretching motion, and she remembered the feel of their strength beneath the palms of her hands.

"He's the one who's dangerous," she murmured as the embers of desire kindled within her.

Her hope that her physical attraction to him would diminish hadn't been answered. In fact, with each passing day she was growing more and more attached to him. Just sitting next to him in the evenings watching television made her happy.

"How long before lunch is ready?" he asked through the screened door as he kicked off his boots on the porch.

"It's ready whenever you are," she replied. "It's just soup and sandwiches."

"I've been mucking out stables all morning." Entering in his stocking feet, he hung his hat on its peg. Then he wiped the streams of sweat from his brow with the sleeve of his shirt leaving a streak of dirt behind. "Think I'll take a quick shower before I eat."

Rachel had never thought the smell of horses, hay and sweat could be so enticing. At this moment, it was acting like a lusty perfume, tantalizing her senses. *It's not safe to have so little resistance to him,* she warned herself.

Logan hadn't continued on through the kitchen but had, instead, paused to let his gaze travel over her. She saw the passion he was stirring within her reflected in his eyes. "I could use someone to scrub my back," he said with a coaxing grin.

Now's your chance to practice some restraint, her inner voice pointed out. She ignored it. "A wife's work is never done," she returned with a teasing mock sigh. Tossing aside the tea towel she'd been holding, she moved toward him.

Grinning, he hooked an arm around her waist. "Did I ever tell you how appetizing you look in a pair of jeans?" he asked as they left the kitchen.

"You don't look so bad yourself," she returned, recalling watching him approaching the house.

His grin broadened. Pausing and turning to face her, he dropped a light kiss on her mouth. "But you look even better out of them."

"So do you," she returned. So much for showing some decorum. Then she glanced up at him. There was amusement in his eyes, but there was also a heat that enfolded her like a wool blanket on a cold winter night. Her legs felt suddenly weak while her heart began to beat double time. *You're in love with him,* her inner voice wailed in dismay. But she didn't care. The way he was looking at her made her believe that this marriage could last forever.

She was still holding that thought as they sat in the kitchen a while later eating slightly stale sandwiches and reheated soup.

"Hank, Wanda and the baby are settled in comfortably now," Logan was saying. "And Wanda has arranged for her sister to come stay with her for a while. So I thought, if you'd like, we'd spend the Fourth of July with my family in Los Angeles and then fly to Copenhagen for that honeymoon I promised you. I was there once. Denmark is beautiful this time of the year."

Rachel experienced a surge of panic. *You knew you were going to have to meet his family sooner or later.* Besides, his mother and stepfather had accepted her.

Reaching across the table, Logan took her hand in his. "My brothers and sister are looking forward to meeting you," he said. He seemed assured that she had nothing to worry about.

I hope he's right, she prayed silently.

Chapter Eleven

"Well, what do you think of my family?" Logan asked.

It was the night of July the third and they were lying in bed in one of the guest rooms at his parents' home in one of the wealthier subdivisions outside Los Angeles. They had flown in that day, and his mother had arranged for the entire family to come for dinner.

Outwardly Rachel had remained calm. Inwardly she'd been on the verge of panic. But the evening had gone well. Logan's half brothers and his half sister and their families had treated her well. None of them, on the surface at least, had appeared to object to her being a member of their family.

"They're very nice," she replied.

"I think Jason has a crush on you," Logan said good-naturedly.

The image of Logan's five-year-old nephew played through Rachel's mind. The boy's father was John, Logan's oldest half brother. With his blond hair and blue eyes, John took after George. In turn, Jason resembled his father except that, while John maintained a sober demeanor at all times, Jason had an impish grin that appeared whenever anything stuck him as funny, which was often. At first the child had watched her with un-abashed curiosity but kept his distance. By the end of the evening, however, he'd stationed himself by her side.

"He's a little charmer," she said. The thought of Logan's nephew caused her to think of his other nephews and nieces. And two of his sisters-in-law were pregnant again. A nagging worry she'd been trying to ignore all evening suddenly surfaced full force.

"My brother brought his family out to the ranch last summer," Logan said with a grin. "Jason in-sisted on being put on a horse. I still have the sad-dle my dad had gotten for me when I was that age, so I pulled it out and took the boy for a ride. Had to saddle him a full-sized horse, but he didn't balk. Sat right up there like he was born to ride."

Rachel was only half listening as a battle raged within her. Ignoring trouble never makes it go away, she reminded herself sternly. Levering her-self up on an elbow, she looked down into Logan's face. The moonlight coming in through the window illuminated his features. "Are you very disappointed?"

He frowned in confusion. "What are you talking about? I thought this evening went very well."

"The evening did," she conceded. For a moment she hesitated, then forced herself to go on. "It was just that seeing all the children and your pregnant sisters-in-law reminded me of our deal. I was supposed to provide you with heirs. So far, I haven't been successful in getting pregnant."

"To be honest, I'm enjoying having you all to myself," he replied, wrapping his arms around her and drawing her close.

Now that she had broached the subject she was tempted to ask him how he would feel if she was never able to get pregnant. But her doctor had told her she was perfectly capable of having children. Besides, the way he was touching her made conversation the last thing she felt like doing right now....

The next day dawned bright and clear.

"A perfect day for a round of golf," Gail said brightly as they sat at the breakfast table. An edge of apology crept into her voice as she glanced at Rachel. "I hope you don't mind. Every year, as a charity function, we have a small local golf tournament at the country club. George is in charge of the officiating, and John and Ted are participating. We'll have to go over for a while, but we don't

have to stay all day. We can use our having to over-
see the preparations for the family picnic and
fireworks we're having here this evening as an excuse to escape right after lunch."

"Logan can show off his beautiful new wife,"
George added with a grin.

"I hope you don't mind," Gail continued
quickly, smiling coaxingly at Rachel. "I've arranged a welcome to the family gift for you. I
wasn't certain if you'd have time to shop before you
came, so I had some outfits that would be appro-
priate for today's outing sent over from one of my
favorite dress shops. I want you to pick whichever
one pleases you the most as a present from George
and me."

Rachel couldn't fault the woman's diplomacy. It
was obvious Gail had guessed Rachel probably
wouldn't have the kind of clothes Logan's wife
should have for such an occasion. And she guessed
right, Rachel conceded, mentally going over her
wardrobe. "That was very thoughtful of you."

"I was counting on your taking Rachel shopping tomorrow," Logan interjected. "I figured
you'd know all the right places."

Gail smiled broadly and reaching across the table, she gave Rachel's hand a comradely squeeze.
"We'll have a ball."

Rachel forced a smile. She might be Logan's
wife, but she still didn't feel comfortable spending
his money. *I'll use my own,* she decided, and her
smile became more relaxed.

* * *

It was midmorning when she, Logan and Gail arrived at the country club. Molly, Logan's sister, came out of the dining room to greet them.

"Everyone is out on the golf course," she said. "I just came in to make certain the brunch is being laid out properly. The first players should be coming in off the course soon, and that means the first group of hungry spectators will be wanting to be fed."

The people passing all nodded or waved to Gail and Molly, and it quickly became obvious to Rachel that Logan's family was very active and well thought of at the club.

"Ted and John were in the first batch," Molly continued, then glancing over her shoulder toward the dining room, she added apologetically, "I just have a couple more things I need to check on."

Before the trio could even say goodbye, she was on her way.

Next, Logan, Rachel and Gail wandered toward a spectator area of the course, and Gail introduced Rachel to several people. *These are the kinds of affairs I used to drive people to,* Rachel mused, as her gaze traveled over the obviously wealthy assemblage. Mentally she again thanked Gail for the designer pants outfit she was wearing. At least she would not be a source of embarrassment to Logan or his family.

This thought was barely formed when the sound of a familiar voice caused every muscle in Rachel's body to tense.

"Well, well, if it isn't Logan and his new wife," Marylin Jennings said, coming up behind Rachel.

Hoping that Marylin wouldn't cause any trouble, Rachel forced a smile and turned toward the woman. Her hopes died an instant death when she saw the maliciousness in the younger woman's eyes.

"You're a little far from home, aren't you?" Logan said to Marylin. His voice was cool and there was a warning in his eyes.

"Grandfather and I are visiting the Baileys, and their grandson Vince insisted we come by and watch him play," she replied in a honey-coated voice.

Rachel had never known Marylin to heed a warning when she had her heart set on revenge, but then, Logan could be very intimidating. Maybe, just this once, the woman would behave, Rachel wished fervently.

Marylin's gaze turned to Rachel. In the same sticky-sweet tone, she said, "You're looking very well. Of course that's only to be expected. You're a lucky woman to have captured Logan for a husband."

Rachel's panic began to subside. It appeared that Marylin was going to behave. She smiled. "I think so."

Marylin's attention remained focused on her.

Feeling the need to say something more, Rachel asked, "How is your grandfather?" It seemed like a polite, innocuous remark.

Malicious amusement suddenly sparkled in Marylin's eyes. It was as if she had been waiting for just this cue. "My grandfather is doing just fine ever since he threw you out of our house," Marylin replied in a voice purposely loud enough for the people standing nearby to hear. "He doesn't have to worry about locking up the family silver any longer."

"You hateful child!" Gail gasped.

"What the devil?" a man's voice demanded from behind.

Rachel glanced over her shoulder. It was John who had spoken. He and Ted, along with a crowd of others, had approached. From the looks on their faces, it was obvious to Rachel that they'd heard what Marylin had said. The blonde's timing had been perfect. With so many witnesses, Marylin's lies would be thoroughly spread among Logan's family's friends and acquaintances by the end of the day.

Her back stiffened. She'd faced this kind of embarrassment before, but it wasn't fair for Logan and his family to be dragged into it. A knot formed in her stomach and bile rose in her throat. They were certain to regret having her as one of them after this.

Suddenly Logan's arm was around her shoulders, holding her protectively.

Gail swung around, searching the faces of the crowd. Finding the one she was looking for she called out, "Justin Parry, you get over here immediately." Then slipping her arm around Rachel's waist, she glared at Marylin.

"I really must be running along now," Marylin said, her voice once again honey-coated.

"You stay right here, young lady," Gail ordered.

A glimmer of fear shone in Marylin's eyes. "I'm hungry," she replied, and began moving away.

In the next instant, Ted and John had flanked her. "It's not polite to walk away when someone wants to speak to you," John admonished.

"What's going on here?" Justin asked, glancing around the group.

Logan's gaze narrowed threateningly on Justin. "Your granddaughter has been viciously attempting to malign my wife. We both know who the 'thief' in your house was, and I will not have unjust lies and innuendos spread about Rachel."

"That girl needs to have a good swift kick and her mouth washed out with soap," Gail added.

"Wouldn't be the first time she's caused innocent people trouble," a female voice muttered in the background. This statement was followed by confirming murmurs.

"But it had better be the last time where my family and friends are concerned," Logan growled.

Justin glanced at Marylin.

Tears welled in the blonde's eyes and the look of an unfairly accused innocent came over her face. "Really, Grandfather, they're overreacting. You know Rachel never liked me. This is all her fault."

"I know very well whose fault it is," Justin replied.

A sly smile began to tilt one corner of Marylin's mouth as Justin turned back toward Rachel. Rachel braced herself for a renewed defense of his granddaughter.

"I apologize to you, and to Logan and his family," Justin said.

Marylin looked as if she'd been slapped. She stomped her foot and her innocent expression gave way to one of pure fury. "Really, Grandfather! She was nothing but a chauffeur and she did spend time in jail. Logan could have done a whole lot better. You men will let a pretty face and good figure make fools of you anytime."

Turning back toward Marylin, Justin shook his head. "I really have spoiled you," he said. Then he took her by the arm and led her toward the exit.

George had joined the group surrounding Rachel; so had both Ted and John's wives. "I'm so sorry about this," Rachel managed to say around the lump in her throat.

"It's not your fault," Logan assured her.

"That little witch should have been caged long ago," John's wife said.

Gail gave Rachel a squeeze. "Let's go inside," she said.

But as both Logan and his mother attempted to urge Rachel toward the clubhouse, she balked. "I can't," she said in a voice near panic.

Logan's hold on her shoulder tightened. "I'll take you home."

Gail gave Rachel another hug, then released her hold on her waist. "We'll see you there in a little while."

"I really am sorry," Rachel repeated weakly as she and Logan walked toward the car. She would have preferred to run, but she had some pride left.

"There is nothing for you to be sorry about," Logan replied.

Rachel paused to glare up at him. How could he be so thick-headed? "I embarrassed you and your family!" she snapped.

He regarded her with an impatient scowl. "*You* didn't embarrass us."

She knew that look. Arguing wouldn't do any good. But as they drove back to the house, there was one thing she knew she had to say to him. When he pulled into the driveway and parked, she laid a restraining hand on his arm before he could get out of the car. "I'm used to living with my past." Tears of anger burned in her eyes. "Sometimes it doesn't seem fair that one small mistake should keep coming back to cause trouble, but it does." She swallowed back the lump that formed in her throat. She'd faced a lot of difficult situations in her life, but the next thing she had to say was the hardest she'd ever had to say. "I will understand if you want out of this marriage. It will no doubt cause you more embarrassment if you remain in it.''

Logan's hands closed around her upper arms, turning her to face him. "I do not want out of this marriage," he said firmly. "You are not an embarrassment to me. You suit me just fine. You fit into my life-style. We get along well. That's more than a lot of couples can claim."

He sounded so practical. But then that was what their marriage was to him—a practical arrangement. *And that's what it should be to me,* she ordered herself for the hundredth time. "I just thought I should offer you the opportunity to get out," she said calmly.

Releasing her, his expression became shuttered. "All right. You have and I've refused it. Now let's go inside and get some lunch. I'm hungry."

Rachel tried to eat but she couldn't. The food lodged in her throat and the walls seemed to close in on her. Finally she put her fork aside and rose. "I think I'll go for a walk."

She was barely halfway across the dining room before Logan caught up with her. He grasped her upper arm and brought her to a halt. "I've been wondering," he said, studying her closely, "what's become of the thick-skinned woman who couldn't wait to tell everyone about her past."

The memory of how her life had been before Logan entered it flashed through her mind. She'd worked hard to keep herself apart from others. It had been safer that way. If no one got close, they couldn't hurt her. But the one thing she'd never admitted to herself was how lonely her private little world had been. "Maybe she just got tired of being on the outside all the time," she heard herself saying. Every muscle in her body tensed. She couldn't believe she'd said that. "Besides," she added quickly, "it's not me I'm so concerned about. It's your family and you."

"My family and I can handle this just fine," he said. He traced the line of her jaw with the tips of his fingers. "And what you've got to keep in mind is that the people who would hold your past against you aren't worth knowing. I guarantee you'll be surprised by how many are willing to give you a chance to be a friend."

She wanted to believe him, but she was afraid. "The surprises I've had in my life have not, as a rule, been pleasant," she replied dryly and strode out of the room.

Standing and staring out the living-room window at the manicured lawn, hot tears filled her eyes. Logan had been one of the few pleasant surprises. She never wanted to do anything that would cause him grief. Silently she promised herself that if he was wrong about the effect this morning's incident would have on his family, she would leave and set him free. *You knew it would be dangerous to start believing that something as good as your marriage to Logan could last,* she chided herself.

"It's time to start rebuilding that thick skin," she muttered.

"I sort of liked the thinner one."

Startled, Rachel swung around to find Logan standing behind her. She'd been so absorbed in her own thoughts she hadn't heard him approaching. "I didn't know you were so light on your feet," she said. "You shouldn't sneak up on someone like that."

"I didn't mean to startle you." He cupped her face in his hands. "Letting people get close to you can be risky. But sometimes it can be worth the risk."

"I'd like to believe you're right," she replied.

"Trust me," he ordered gently. Then he kissed her lightly on the tip of her nose and drew her into his arms.

Standing in his protective embrace, she admitted to herself that she *did* trust him. It was scary how much a part of her he had become. And she knew that he would always be a part of her no matter what happened.

She drew a shaky breath. She fervently hoped he was right about his family's response to what Marylin had said.

And he was.

When Gail returned home that afternoon, Rachel again apologized to her for being a source of embarrassment. Gail quickly assured Rachel that there was nothing to apologize for. The sincerity in her voice convinced Rachel that she was telling the truth.

That evening the rest of the family was as friendly as they had been the night before, and Rachel began to relax.

But the next day she soon learned that not everyone had put the incident to rest. She and Gail were at one of the better dress shops in town. To Rachel's chagrin, Logan had given his mother his credit card with explicit instructions that she was to see that Rachel used it extensively. And Gail was doing just that. Their car was loaded with boxes of shoes and bags of new clothes.

"This will be the very last stop," Gail promised as they entered the store. "They have an exquisite evening dress here that I know is perfect for you."

Rachel had learned early in the day that it was useless to try to dissuade Gail once the woman had her mind set, so she simply followed in her wake.

They were in one of the booths in the dressing area when two other women entered the booth next to theirs.

"I felt so sorry for Gail," one of them was saying in a catty tone that belied her claim of sympathy. "It must be devastating to her to have her son married to an ex-convict."

"Are you sure you got the facts right?" the second woman asked, her interest obviously piqued.

"Of course. Marylin Jennings told me herself," the woman replied in a tone that suggested she was offended at having her word questioned.

"That big bag of wind," Gail seethed under her breath. "I'm going in there to give her a piece of my mind."

Rachel laid a restraining hand on Gail's arm. Swallowing back the bile that had risen to her throat, she said, "It won't do any good—I know from experience. As far as it goes, she does have the facts straight, and you'll have to admit to that if she asks."

Gail scowled. "Well, people who gossip had better be certain their own homes are full of paragons," she said in a voice loud enough to carry into the next booth.

Two simultaneous gasps let them know her remark had been heard and her voice recognized. Almost immediately there was the sound of a quick exit from the adjoining booth.

"If I had known my past would cause you and your family so much trouble, I would never have married Logan," Rachel said, staring at the wall that separated them from the next booth.

Gail gave her a hug. "Don't be silly," she admonished. "The people who count will give you a chance. That woman who was talking is a notorious gossip. When George married me, she went around proclaiming that I was nothing but a gold digger. She claimed that my first husband was a poor farmer whom I'd left heartbroken and alone to run off with George because George was wealthy. You can't let people like that rule your life."

"You're right," Rachel agreed. Still, she couldn't help wondering if, beneath her reassuring surface, Gail didn't wish Logan had chosen a wife with a less blemished past.

The next day Rachel and Logan left for Copenhagen. Rachel breathed a sigh of relief as they boarded the plane. But during the flight the thought that they might run into some of Logan's wealthy friends there crossed her mind. She told herself it was silly to worry about such a thing. Still, she remained tense.

Logan's hand suddenly closed over hers. Looking up at him, she saw him smiling at her with that crooked smile of his. "Shall we behave like an old married couple and spend all our time sightseeing?" he asked, leaning close to her ear so that his breath teased her skin. "Or shall we behave like newlyweds and never leave our room?" he finished in a playfully coaxing tone as he nipped her earlobe.

The touch of his hand warmed her and the feel of his lips as he left a trail of light kisses from her earlobe to her neck made her want to forget everything but him. "A little of each would be nice," she replied.

"A little of each it is," he agreed, kissing her on the lips as if sealing a bargain. Then, continuing to hold her hand, he leaned back in his seat and went to sleep.

For a long time, she sat watching him. He, his mother and his family were all willing to put the incident at the country club behind them. *And I should, too,* Rachel told herself. In a way what had happened should be a source of relief. Her past was now out in the open and his family was still willing to accept her.

Abruptly a shiver of fear shook her. It all seemed too good to be true.

I've had enough bad luck in my life for a dozen lifetimes, she reasoned. Something good was due to come her way. She'd just never expected to find anything as good as Logan.

Chapter Twelve

"All fantasies have to come to an end," Rachel muttered. The summer had passed. It was late October now, and the weather had grown cold once again. But nothing could compare to the chill that passed through her as she stood staring at the phone.

Gail had just called.

During Logan and Rachel's stay in Copenhagen, Logan had spoiled Rachel outrageously. He'd even insisted on buying her an extravagantly expensive emerald-and-diamond necklace with earrings to match. But it had been his attentiveness that had really mattered to her. When they were out sight-seeing, he would hold her hand. Sometimes, he would walk with his arm around her back, his hand resting at her waist. He took her to the finest restaurants and teased her about eating heartily because he had a very strenuous schedule for the rest of the night. Then he'd take her back to the hotel and make love to her with a passion that thrilled her.

By the time they had returned to the ranch, she'd convinced herself that this marriage could last forever. She'd even been able to put the incident at the country club out of her mind. But now the memories flooded back.

Gail had called about Thanksgiving. "I know Logan is concerned about your feelings," Gail had said. "But I can assure you that the Fourth of July business is old news. The family has always gotten together for a big Thanksgiving dinner. I do hope you and Logan will reconsider and come."

Rachel had promised she would speak to Logan about it. Now she wondered what she would say to him.

Obviously he'd told his mother they wouldn't be attending. But he hadn't even mentioned Thanksgiving to her, hadn't, in fact, given her the opportunity to choose whether or not she wanted to face the possibility of again being the brunt of unpleasant gossip. *Because it's not just my feelings he's concerned about.* She couldn't fault him for not wanting to expose his family to another ugly scene. But because of her he was avoiding them.

"And one day he'll regret giving them up for me. Then he'll begin to regret ever having met me," she informed the grim image staring back at her from the mirror. As she stood there, a horrifying thought struck her. Maybe he already was. A couple of times in the past few days she had noticed him watching her guardedly. Logan was a good man, the kind of man who would stick by a bargain for better or worse. Her jaw tensed as her gaze locked with that of her image in the mirror. "You know what you have to do."

She spent the rest of the morning packing. She'd left a lot of places in her life. Most she'd been happy to say goodbye to. But just the thought of leaving here was tearing her apart. "It'd be worse to stay and watch Logan start to wish he'd never laid eyes on me," she reasoned. The pain that would cause was something she couldn't even imagine.

She slipped off her engagement ring and put it in the jeweler's box that contained the emerald necklace and earrings. She hadn't married Logan for profit. The designer dresses she packed in a box he could send to his mother. She was fairly certain they could be altered to fit the other women in the family.

But her wedding ring, as well as the boots, jeans and hat he'd bought her when she first came to the ranch, she kept. "Some mementos of one of the best times in my life," she murmured as she closed her trunk. "And that's that," she added with finality.

Hot tears burned in her eyes. "I'll have a good cry after I'm gone," she promised herself. It had been a long time since she'd cried over anything the fates had dealt her. But this she would cry over. "Not now, though," she ordered herself. She would leave with the same dignity with which she had arrived.

Going into the kitchen, she glanced at the clock. A rush of panic swept through her. Logan would be coming back to the house for lunch any moment now. She would tell him then that she wanted to leave and insist that he take her into Billings this afternoon. "I can do this," she told herself. "I have to."

She had just heated the soup and finished making him a sandwich when she saw him coming toward the house. She stood frozen at the window, watching him, taking in every detail. *You'd be better off trying to put him entirely out of your mind instead of storing up images of him to carry away with you,* her inner voice warned. *When I'm gone, I'll forget him,* she vowed. But at this moment she could not keep herself from indulging in one last, long look. The memory of waking in the mornings in the secure warmth of his embrace entered her mind. She'd forget him, but it was going to take a while.

"Weather's warming a mite," he said with a grin as he entered and hung his hat and coat on their pegs. "Thought you might like to go for a ride this afternoon."

Her stomach knotted. *Say it!* she ordered herself. "Actually I would." Her throat felt as if it was going to constrict. "I'd like for you to take me into Billings," she finished levelly.

He grinned. "Forget something when we were there on Saturday?"

"No." Her stomach twisted more. *Get this over with,* she commanded herself. Her hands began to ball into fists as she fought for control. She shoved them into her pockets. She was determined to appear calm. "I've been feeling restless lately. I'd forgotten how long the winters here were. You've been really good to me and I appreciate that, but this marriage hasn't worked out exactly like I'd hoped. I've been thinking that it would be best to call it off now before we start getting on each other's nerves."

Logan's grin had been replaced by stunned surprise when she started speaking. That had been followed by a flash of anger. Now he was regarding her with the cool, calculating expression she remembered from their first encounter. "My dad always said it wasn't any use trying to keep a woman when she wanted to go. How soon will you be ready to leave?"

The knot in her stomach twisted even more. He hadn't shown any sign of regret. "I'm packed," she replied, fighting to keep her voice steady. "We can leave as soon as you've eaten."

For a moment he remained silent. Then he shrugged. "I'll be finished in a few minutes."

"Fine." Unable to face him any longer, she headed toward the door. "I'll wait for you in the living room," she tossed over her shoulder as she made her hasty retreat. But she didn't stop in the living room. She continued on through the house to the bedroom she'd used when she'd first arrived. She needed a moment or two behind a closed door.

She was shaking by the time she reached the sought-after sanctuary. Kicking the door closed, she crossed to the window and stared out at the bleak landscape. He didn't care. She hadn't expected him to beg her to stay. But she had thought he might show a small amount of regret that their marriage hadn't worked out. "He's probably breathing one huge sigh of relief," she muttered. "Well, at least this should make forgetting him easier."

A sharp knock on the door caused her to jump. She jerked around just as Logan entered. "Ready so soon?" she asked dryly. Clearly he couldn't wait to be rid of her.

"No," came his gruff reply. His jaw hardened. "Truth is I've gotten used to having you around. And you're right about the winters. They are long and they can get lonely. If you're restless we can take a few trips. I'll hire a second regular hand. There's a bunkhouse that can be easily fixed up for use. Then I'll be able to get away more often."

She stared at him in stunned disbelief. He was asking her to stay. He was even willing to make concessions. The thought that he might have learned to honestly care for her entered her mind. Then she remembered how coolly he'd accepted the news of her leaving. He was only doing this because he was tired of living alone. After a while he'd realize what he was giving up and then he'd resent her. "It can't work. It's best if I leave now," she replied stiffly.

Cynicism etched itself into his features. "I guess you figure you've given me enough of your time to earn that settlement we agreed on."

He was accusing her of having married him for his money! Anger brought a scarlet flush to her cheeks. "I have no intention of taking anything from you. I left the clothes you bought me. You can give them to your mother. I'm sure they can be altered for the other women in the family. As for the jewels, I left them on the bureau." A hurt like none she'd ever felt before mingled with her anger. Suddenly she didn't want anything to remind her of him. "And you can have this back, too." Pulling her wedding ring off her finger, she threw it at him. So much for exiting with dignity, she thought. Afraid he might see the tears of pain forming in her eyes, she turned her back to him and feigned interest in the view beyond the window. "Whenever you're ready, we can leave."

"Rachel, I'm sorry," he said. Frustration entered his voice. "I'm just trying to understand. When I left the house this morning, I could have sworn you were happy here."

She heard him moving toward her. Panic filled her. Her control had already slipped once. If he touched her, it might very likely slip again. She had to get out of there. She turned toward him. "Things change," she said coldly. "Now, can we be on our way?"

She tried to edge past him, but his hands closed around her upper arms, pinning her in front of him. "I've always tried to follow my father's advice, but I'm finding it difficult just to stand back and let you walk away. I guess my ego wasn't ready for this. But don't worry, I won't try to hold you against your will." His gaze narrowed on her. "We can leave as soon as you look me in the eye and tell me one more time you honestly want to go."

His touch was having a seriously weakening effect on her. I can do this, she told herself, but the words stuck in her throat. Jerking free, she took a step back from him. "Stop it, Logan. I'm trying to do the right thing! I have to leave." She couldn't believe she'd blurted that out. She needed to get away from him. She had to regain control. She started toward the door.

"No, you don't." Again he stopped her escape, blocking her with his body. "I want to know why you think you have to leave."

Her jaw tensed. "I don't *think,* I *know.*" She glared at him in frustration. She couldn't believe he wasn't already feeling at least a twinge of regret for having to stay away from his family because of her. "And you know it, too."

His hands again closed around her upper arms. "I don't *know* anything," he growled. "You're not making any sense, Rachel."

Why was he making this so difficult? She tried to jerk free, but this time his hold was too strong. Her tears threatened again. Panic swept through her. She couldn't cry in front of him. She had some pride left. "You're the one who's not making any sense," she said through clenched teeth. "I know about Thanksgiving." She swallowed down the lump that suddenly filled her throat. "And I don't blame you for trying to protect your family from any further scandal by keeping me away from them. I don't want to cause them any further grief, either. But you have to realize that if you stay away from them because of me, eventually you'll begin to resent me, maybe even hate me. I'm not going to stick around for that." Her chin trembled. "You're a good man, Logan James," she said softly. "The best I've ever known. I know if you set your mind to it, you can find a wife who's more socially acceptable, and one you can love."

There, she'd said it! She couldn't face him any longer. Her gaze dropped to the third button on his shirt. She breathed a tired, wistful sigh. "I know none of this has worked out the way you'd hoped. I haven't even given you an heir." Now tears flooded her eyes. Frantic, she tried to pull free once again.

Logan's hold only tightened. "I don't give a damn about an heir. And it was you I've been trying to protect. My family can handle a little gossip. It's only you and me it's aimed at, anyway, and I couldn't care less what a bunch of old busybodies say. But the effect the incident at the clubhouse had on you scared me. I was afraid I was going to lose you. I thought you'd be tougher, but you were suddenly talking about a divorce."

"I didn't want you to feel that you were stuck with a wife who was an embarrassment to you and your family," she returned. He'd said he was protecting her. He'd said he was afraid of losing her. He'd even said he didn't care about an heir. She wanted to believe him.

Releasing her arms, he cupped her face gently in his hands. "You're not an embarrassment and I want very much to be stuck with you."

There was a warmth in the dark depths of his eyes that caused her legs to weaken. But still she was frightened. "I've had a lot of disappointments in my life, Logan, a lot of disillusionments, and I've survived them. But if I stay and you change your mind about me, if you get bored with me or frustrated I can't give you an heir, I'm not sure I could survive that."

He looked hard into her face. "I can't imagine ever being bored with you. As for children, if we can't have any of our own, we can adopt. It's you who is important to me, Rachel. I'm in love with you."

Her heart began to pound wildly. "You're in love with me?" she repeated, worried that maybe she had wanted to hear him say that so badly she'd imagined it.

"I have been for a long time." He grinned coaxingly. "I can't promise I'll be the perfect husband. We're bound to have disagreements. But I'll always love you. You can take my word for that."

He honestly loved her! He'd given her his word, and Logan James was a man of his word. Happiness bubbled up inside her. "Logan," she said softly. Tenderly she stroked his jaw. "I love you, too."

He laughed then, a triumphant, joyful laugh. In the next instant he was scooping her up in his arms. "I've got a much better way of spending the afternoon than going out for a ride," he said, carrying her toward their room.

Later as she lay snuggled in his arms, Rachel breathed a contented sigh. Then her stomach growled, reminding her that neither she nor Logan had eaten lunch. Pushing herself up on an elbow, she kissed him lightly. "I'll go make us some sandwiches."

But when she tried to leave, his hold on her tightened. "Just lie with me a little longer," he requested gruffly. "I felt as if I'd been kicked in the stomach by a mule when you said you were going to leave. I still need a little reassurance that this is real."

Gently she traced his forehead, cheeks and mouth with her fingertips. "I have to admit I'm finding this a little difficult to believe myself. I never thought I'd ever find anyone like you.''

He grinned crookedly. ''From the first moment I saw you standing at attention beside Justin's Rolls, I wanted you. Scared the hell out of me. No woman had ever affected me so strongly before.''

Recalling how coolly he'd regarded her that day, she frowned at him. ''You were very good at hiding your feelings.''

''I'd always promised myself I'd never play the fool where a woman was concerned.'' He kissed her shoulder lightly. ''But I was sure I was doing exactly that when I offered you the job at my ranch. Of course I told myself it would be a cure for me. I figured you'd take one look at the isolation out here and run. But you didn't.''

''And I thought you were a man who always knew precisely what he was doing,'' she teased, surprised by these confessions but enjoying them.

Remembered frustration showed in his eyes. ''Not where you were concerned. You were good at hiding it, but I'd caught a glimpse of the hurt Justin had caused you. I knew that under that tough exterior you presented to the world there was a softer soul. But those barriers you'd built around yourself were sturdy. There were times when I thought I'd never get through them.'' His hand moved caressingly along her back and the warmth returned to his eyes. ''I'd always prided myself on my patience, but there was one time when I lost it entirely. I even told myself to give up, that you were never going to let me get close to you. But instead, I went out and tried to ride Dancer."

The day he'd gotten thrown from the horse came back to Rachel's mind with vivid clarity. The fear she'd felt then washed through her again. "You nearly got your neck broken."

He grinned. "But it was worth it to see the concern in your eyes. After that, I was willing to take you for my wife any way I could get you—even if it meant cutting a bargain. I was determined to teach you to love me."

"You succeeded very well," she assured him, forgetting about lunch as his touch rekindled desire....

*   *   *   *   *

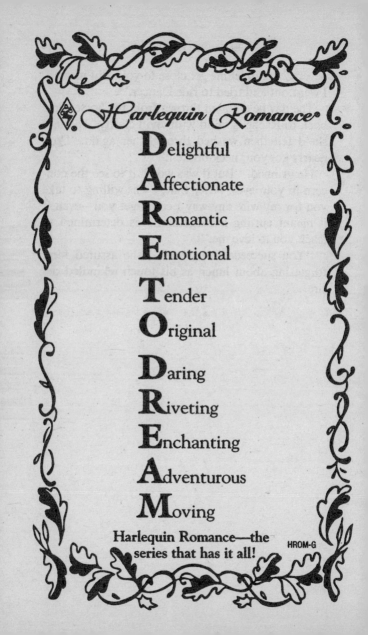

Harlequin Romance®

Delightful

Affectionate

Romantic

Emotional

Tender

Original

Daring

Riveting

Enchanting

Adventurous

Moving

Harlequin Romance—the series that has it all!

HROM-G

HARLEQUIN PRESENTS®

HARLEQUIN PRESENTS
men you won't be able to resist falling in love with...

HARLEQUIN PRESENTS
women who have feelings just like your own...

HARLEQUIN PRESENTS
powerful passion in exotic international settings...

HARLEQUIN PRESENTS
intense, dramatic stories that will keep you turning
to the very last page...

HARLEQUIN PRESENTS
The world's bestselling romance series!

Harlequin® Historical

If you're a serious fan of historical romance,
then you're in luck!

Harlequin Historicals brings you
stories by bestselling authors, rising new stars
and talented first-timers.

Ruth Langan & Theresa Michaels
Mary McBride & Cheryl St.John
Margaret Moore & Merline Lovelace
Julie Tetel & Nina Beaumont
Susan Amarillas & Ana Seymour
Deborah Simmons & Linda Castle
Cassandra Austin & Emily French
Miranda Jarrett & Suzanne Barclay
DeLoras Scott & Laurie Grant…

You'll never run out of favorites.

Harlequin Historicals…they're too good to miss!

HH-GEN

SPECIAL EDITION

Stories of love and life, these powerful
novels are tales that you can identify with—
romances with "something special" added in!

Fall in love with the stories of authors such
as **Nora Roberts, Diana Palmer, Ginna Gray**
and many more of your special favorites—as
well as wonderful new voices!

Special Edition brings you
entertainment for the heart!

SSE-GEN

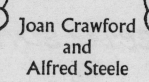

Joan Crawford
and
Alfred Steele

Ms. Crawford had worked as a laundress, waitress and shop girl before she won a Charleston contest and was discovered in a Broadway chorus by MGM. A nationwide publicity contest for a suitable screen name resulted in "Joan Crawford."

Crawford was the least-liked actress in Hollywood. Everyone from Bette Davis to her adopted daughter, Christina, had problems with her. In the thirties Crawford became quite eccentric. She suffered from claustrophobia, a fear of flying and was fanatical about hygiene. She scrubbed her own floors, even as a star.

Her fourth marriage was to Alfred Steele, board chairman of Pepsi, in 1956. She became active in publicizing Pepsi-Cola and was elected to the board of directors. Steele died in his sleep from a heart attack in 1959. She never remarried.

B-JOAN